THE
DADA CAPER

ROSS H. SPENCER

AVON
PUBLISHERS OF BARD, CAMELOT AND DISCUS BOOKS

THE DADA CAPER is an original publication of Avon
Books. This work has never before appeared in book
form.

AVON BOOKS
A division of
The Hearst Corporation
959 Eighth Avenue
New York, New York 10019

Library of Congress Catalog Card Number: 77-99228
ISBN: 0-380-01839-X

First Avon Printing, February, 1978

AVON TRADEMARK REG. U.S. PAT. OFF. AND IN
OTHER COUNTRIES, MARCA REGISTRADA,
HECHO EN U.S.A.

Printed in Canada

This book is dedicated to Viola Manak who contributed 1 excellent typing job, 22,876 magnificent exhortations, 51,017 ominous frowns, 78,949 blood-curdling threats and more than 3,000,000 tears. These were important but it was her laughter that helped most. She laughed my way through it.

... Oncet I knowed a feller what said he could never find no excuse for stupidity ... he better keep looking ... I think he needs one. ...

MONROE D. UNDERWOOD

❈

Kellis J. Ammson of the Ammson Private Detective Agency stared at me with bulging gray eyes.

They were incredulous eyes underlined by dark half-moons.

They were the eyes of a man who has just spent a night in a haunted house.

Kellis J. Ammson said oh dear great flaming sweet and merciful eternal flaming Lord Savior Jesus flaming Christ Al-flaming-mighty.

I didn't say anything.

I don't know much about that kind of stuff.

If there were any doubts that Kellis J. Ammson was very unhappy he dispelled them then and there.

Kellis J. Ammson said I am very flaming unhappy.

I shrugged.

I said well.

Kellis J. Ammson held a shaking silver lighter to an imported aromatic bamboo-tipped cigarette.

He said Chance there are a couple flaming things you ought to know.

I shrugged.

I said shoot.

Kellis J. Ammson laughed.

Bitterly.

He said I've considered that.

I held a paper match to a badly bent Camel.

I watched a sparrow come roaring in to a full-flaps landing on the window ledge.

I studied the baby-blue nylon carpeting.

I waited.

Kellis J. Ammson surged forward in his four-hundred-dollar black genuine-leather swivel chair.

He looked like an enormous beetle out of a Japanese science-fiction movie.

He slammed his big hands flat on the top of his sixteen-hundred-dollar hand-carved Philippine mahogany desk.

The three-carat diamond on his left hand sparkled coldly.

So did the two-carat diamond on his right hand.

Kellis J. Ammson had a very big thing for diamonds.

He spoke softly.

With a great throbbing intensity.

He said Chance when you are working on a flaming divorce case the very first flaming thing you should never do is grab the flaming house detective and go busting into a flaming hotel room and take pictures of Mr. Kenneth Williams making love to his flaming wife.

He said you see Chance what you are supposed to do is take pictures of Mr. Kenneth Williams making love to somebody else's flaming wife.

He said oh flaming Heavenly Father.

Fervently.

I shrugged.

I am very good at shrugging.

I can just shrug up a storm.

I said look Mr. Ammson.

I said Williams met this chick in the hotel lounge.

10

I said he got her looped.

I said he took her upstairs.

I said it looked just like the old routine.

I said how was I to know she was Mrs. Williams?

I said my God I didn't know Mrs. Williams from a side of beef.

Kellis J. Ammson rolled his tortured gray eyes upward.

He frightened me when he did that.

I always expected him to speak in tongues.

He said if you had taken the flaming time to call in yesterday afternoon you would have learned that Mrs. Williams pulled us off the flaming case yesterday flaming morning.

He said they were about to be flaming reconciled.

I said boy you ain't kidding.

I said how flaming reconciled can you get?

I said you should have seen it.

I said that house dick nearly blew his flaming mind.

Kellis J. Ammson threw up his hands.

He shuddered.

He said I wonder how flaming much they'll sue for.

I shrugged.

It was one of my very best shrugs.

I really got my shoulders into it.

I said well gee whiz what's all the excitement about?

I said I forgot to load the goddam camera anyway.

Kellis J. Ammson pursed his lips.

Judiciously.

He nodded.

Sagaciously.

He said I see.

Understandingly.

I said hey that Mrs. Williams sure looks like a swinger.

Kellis J. Ammson sighed.

Martyredly.

He said you know Chance I've been itching to get back into flaming harness.

11

He said this flaming desk is no place for a flaming old war-horse like me.

He said I like to be out where it's all happening.

He said I'm going to team up with Gino Scarletti and hit the flaming bricks again.

I said I don't know Gino Scarletti.

Kellis J. Ammson said Gino is a flaming good man.

He said very flaming tough.

He crushed his cigarette into a white ceramic ashtray not much bigger than a turkey platter.

He drummed the desk top with impatient fingertips.

He said mmmmmmmmm.

Melodiously.

He said I think there was some other flaming thing.

He shuffled through some papers.

He said oh yes.

He handed me a check.

He said you're fired.

The sparrow on the window ledge took off into a strong crosswind.

... oncet I knowed three fellers went in business for theyselves ... didn't do too good ... one got a heart attack ... one committed suicide ... other one got married....

MONROE D. UNDERWOOD

Chance Purdue.
That is my name.
Private detective.
That was my occupation.
I handle anything.
That was my slogan.
Room 506 Braddock Building.
That was my address.
One-year lease.
Three hundred a month.
That was my mistake.

Betsy would breeze into the office about eleven in the morning.

Almost every day.

Betsy worked nights usually.

She would sit in the client's chair.

After she had dusted it.

With wild swooping motions.

So I would know that she knew nobody had sat in it.

Betsy would lean back and cross her long legs.

Betsy wore very short skirts.

And black underclothing.

Most of the time.

She would say how goes it Philo?

I would shrug.

I would say oh just great.

Betsy would say how good is just great?

I would say well right now I am running down a few missing space capsules for NASA.

14

Betsy would toss her head.
Her blonde hair would shimmer.
Her pale blue eyes would twinkle.
She would say horsecrap.
Then she would say I'll take you to lunch.
I would say okay.

❧

We would go to Donelli's.

Betsy wasn't much on Italian food but she was crazy about red and white checked tablecloths.

Betsy would have a salad and an order of rye toast and a brandy ice.

I would have a steak sandwich and a green chartreuse and three black coffees.

Betsy would say how are you ever going to handle three hundred a month office rent?

I would shrug.

Just a run-of-the-mill shrug.

I would say look I don't know everything.

Betsy would say it would be much easier if you moved in with me.

I would shake my head emphatically.

I would say no way.

Betsy would frown.

She would say why not?

I would say because you're a whore.

Betsy would say dammit Chance can't you ever say call girl?

I would shrug.

Betsy would say you told me it wasn't important.

I would say it isn't.

I would say it's that goddam telephone that's important.

I would say that goddam telephone would put me in the cracker shop.

Betsy would say should I have it disconnected?

I would say not until I get a client.

We would go on that way.

When I had been in business a couple of weeks a pudgy woman came in.

She got right down to brass tacks.

She wanted me to guard her Afghan hound for three days.

So it wouldn't get pregnant.

She said Lollipop is very receptive on the eleventh and twelfth and thirteenth days.

I said I never heard of a dog that could read a calendar.

The pudgy woman threw her hands to her mouth.

She tittered.

She said oh gracious no.

She said I am not speaking of days of the month.

She said I refer to days of the heat period.

The pudgy woman said it comes twice a year.

I said well that may be true where Afghan hounds are concerned.

18

I said but it doesn't apply to Airedales.

I said I had an Airedale once.

I said that sonofagun was in heat all the time.

I said boy he sure was horny.

The pudgy woman said I was thinking of females.

I said so was my Airedale.

I sent her over to the Ammson Private Detective Agency.

I said Ammson specializes in cases of this type.

. . . I been so busy counting opportunities
I ain't had time to use any. . . .

MONROE D. UNDERWOOD

The next morning a tall skinny guy came in.
He had wild eyes.
He was smoking a goofy-looking pipe.
He told me he was a detective.
He asked for a job.
I said what's your name?
He said Sherlock Holmes.
I said I would have bet on it.
He said Purdue between us we can lay Professor Moriarty by the heels.
I said is that rascal up to his old tricks?
He said baby you better believe it.
I sent him over to the Ammson Private Detective Agency.
I said Ammson is always looking for good men.
I heard later that Ammson hired him.
As my replacement.

*... friend of mine got an opportunity to
drive a nitroglycerine truck to Alaska...
they named a new canyon after him....*

MONROE D. UNDERWOOD

At the end of the week a woman came puffing into my
office.

She had the demeanor of a Union Pacific four-six-two
steam locomotive.

She had the body to go with it.

And the voice.

She slammed her purse onto my desk.

She crashed into the client's chair.

She said my name is Edna Willock.

I said you got a clear board Edna.

Edna Willock said I want you to follow my husband.

I said is he on the wrong track?

She said he sure is.

She said he tells me lies.

I said maybe we can derail him.

She said he shouldn't tell me lies.

She said he's the preacher at Holy Trinity Gospel
Joshua and Saint James.

21

I said I know an engineer on the Chicago Milwaukee Saint Paul and Pacific.

She said he simply got to quit lying.

She said he tells me he is going to see the Cubs play ball tomorrow.

I said how do you know he isn't?

Edna Willock banged seventy-five dollars down on my desk top.

She said the Cubs are in New York.

She leaned back and shoved her cowcatcher jaw in my direction.

She said that's how I know.

I said I'll tail him like a caboose.

Edna Willock said you seem to have trains on your mind.

She chugged out of my office.

...when you get right down to it just about any old opportunity beats hell out of no opportunity at all....

MONROE D. UNDERWOOD

�֎

The next morning was clear and bright blue.

It would have been a great day for a ball game.

I parked up the block from Edna Willock's house at eleven o'clock.

At eleven-thirty a guy pulled out of her driveway.

He was driving a '75 brown Lincoln Continental with a busted taillight.

Four blocks south he turned west on Irving Park Road.

Wrigley Field was to the east.

So was New York.

Right away I knew he didn't have baseball on his mind.

At four-thirty I broke contact.

I headed for Wallace's tavern.

Wallace sat on a stool behind the bar.

He was glowering at Old Dad Underwood.

Wallace waddled to the tap and drew a beer for me.

He said I am going to sell this joint and move to Utah where I will grow carrots.

23

Old Dad Underwood said oncet I knowed a feller what made a fortune growing carrots.

He said this feller growed carrots twelve feet long.

He said it took three men to carry one.

He said they sliced them up with band saws.

He said they was a bitch to get out of the ground.

He said I think they was hybrids or something.

I said I don't believe they grow a lot of carrots in Utah.

Wallace smiled slyly.

He said so there you are.

He said already I don't got no competition.

He said a man got to be on the alert for chances like this.

During my second beer I called Edna Willock.

I said kiddo you better sit down.

I said your old man is sure some kind of operator.

I said he made ten stops.

I said a couple of them took only fifteen minutes.

I said what's more he is still at it.

I said he ought to be in the Olympics.

I said if he keeps this up he won't be alive when the Cubs get back.

I said does that ring your bell?

Edna Willock whistled.

She said what kind of car is he driving?

I said a '75 brown Lincoln Continental.

I said with a busted taillight.

Edna Willock wheezed like a Union Pacific four-six-two steam locomotive.

She said I want my money back.

She said you have been following our insurance man.

... dogs is man's best friend ... man ain't
nobody's. ...

MONROE D. UNDERWOOD

❈

I drove over to Betsy's apartment on Kelvin Avenue.
When I got out of my car a big hairy dog broke loose
from a woman down the street.
He came bounding up to me.
He was drooling.
He locked his front legs around me.
I struggled.
I said down boy.
When the woman got there she was breathing hard
and swearing softly.
She said now you stop that Bonzo you naughty thing.
She pulled Bonzo away from me.
She said I am very sorry sir.
I said forget it.
I said it's been that kind of day.
She shook a finger at Bonzo.
She said what will this gentleman ever think of you?
I said I think he is an Airedale.

She said you must know a lot about dogs.
I said I know a lot about Airedales.
The lady smiled sweetly.
She had perfect white teeth.
She said my name is Mary Bright.
She said I live just down the street.
She said next door to Mama Rosa's grocery store.
I said I figured you lived just down the street.
Mary Bright said how could you tell?
I said I'm a detective.
I said but I didn't know your name was Mary Bright.
Mary Bright ran a pink tongue over soft red lips.
She said well we learn something every day.
She said we are never too old to learn.
When she walked away I noticed that her slacks were very tight.
Bonzo kept looking back at me.

*... if we didn't have twicet as many tele-
phones we wouldn't have half as much
trouble. ...*

MONROE D. UNDERWOOD

❧

Betsy let me in.
She said I just happened to be looking out.
She said you nearly got it.
I said you ain't just whistling Dixie.
I said she better take that goddam dog to a psychiatrist.
Betsy said I'm not talking about the dog.
She said do you want a drink or a cold shower?
I shrugged.
I said what I really had in mind was a hundred bucks.
Betsy said well there go the day's profits.
She took me by the hand.
She led me into her bedroom.
She gave me five twenty-dollar bills from a dresser
drawer.
She removed my sports coat and threw it on a chair.
She unbuttoned my shirt.
She kissed me.
She said you poor baby.

27

She said baby needs soothing.
I shrugged.
I said okay.
My shirt landed on my sports coat.
The goddam telephone rang.
When Betsy hung up she said stick around.
She said I'll be back in an hour or so.
I said in an hour or so I can be drunk at Wallace's.

I didn't go to Wallace's.
I stopped at Spud's Place.
The television was out of focus.
The beer was lukewarm.
The bartender was going to sleep on his feet.
I went home.
I read the feature story in an *Eagles* magazine.
I fell asleep on the couch.
The telephone woke me up about nine o'clock.
Betsy said I called you at Wallace's a dozen times.
I said I wasn't at Wallace's.
Betsy said I think I got that figured out already.
I said I was at Spud's Place.
Betsy said who is Spud?
I said he was too tired to tell me.
Betsy said I have something for you.
I said well bring it around when it stops smoking.
Betsy said not that you idiot.

She said business.
She said I'm sending you a client.
She said a girl I know.
I said will she keep until morning?
Betsy said she'll be in your office at nine-thirty.
I said thanks sweetie.
Betsy said her name is Candi Yakozi.
I said nobody could be named Candi Yakozi.
Betsy said good-night Philo.

Candi Yakozi was about five-five in her four-inch spike heels.

She had dark brown hair and eyes to match.

She had a pug nose and a bee-stung lower lip and an intimidating bosom.

Her purple dress was so tight I could make out her hysterectomy scar.

She was twenty-five maybe.

She was also thirty-five maybe.

She said you are Chance Purdue.

I said I know it.

Candi Yakozi said I am Betsy's friend.

She said my name is Candi Yakozi.

She plummeted into the client's chair.

She bounced around some.

Her hysterectomy scar rippled.

When she was comfortable she said where should I begin?

I shrugged.

I said the beginning?

Candi Yakozi smiled.

There was a deep dimple in her right cheek.

She said I'm not sure where the beginning began.

She said it could have been the middle before I even found out.

She said which would make it the beginning for me in spite of it being already the middle for him.

She said I mean as far as I am concerned what with me not really knowing it was the middle instead of the beginning and everything like that.

She took a very interesting deep breath.

She said you understand of course.

I nodded my professional reassurance.

It turned out there was a man watching Candi Yakozi.
She told me she couldn't understand why.
I could understand why.
What I couldn't understand was why she couldn't
understand why.
I didn't go into it.
Candi Yakozi told me she was married.
She told me she hadn't seen her husband in several
months.
She told me he was in Montana or Arkansas.
She said I'm not sure which.
She said they are so close together and all.
I said well that's geography for you.
Candi Yakozi scowled a perplexed scowl.
She said yes.
I said so tell me about the man who is watching you.
She said well it's always when it's dark outside.
She said like at night and things.

She said he walks up and down across the street.

She said every so often a guy in a car stops to talk with him.

I said what kind of car is it?

She said oh it is sort of big and black.

She said like in the gangster movies.

I said I will make a note of that.

I made a note of that.

I said what does he look like?

She said who?

She thought about it.

She said oh him.

She said he is medium-sized and he smokes cigarettes.

I said ah ha.

I said why haven't you called the cops?

She said I have more confidence in private detectives.

She said besides they are so sexy.

She said I know because I read a lot of private detective stories.

She said what do you read?

I said mostly letters from collection agencies.

I said those and *Eagles* magazine.

She said what is *Eagles* magazine?

I said it's a magazine about World War I aviators.

She said are World War I aviators as sexy as private detectives?

I said not recently.

I said tell me about this man.

Candi Yakozi stood up and stretched.

She walked to the window.

She said there is a sparrow on your window ledge.

I said I know.

I said he follows me around.

She said what's his name?

I shrugged.

I said Winston probably.

She said why Winston?

I shrugged.

I said I got to call him something.

I said why don't you sit down?

Candi Yakozi sat down.

She said I get like all cramped up while sitting down.

She said you see I prefer lying down to sitting down.

I said I see.

She said as a matter of fact I prefer lying down to standing up.

She said do you like lying down?

I shrugged.

I said oh it'll do.

I said about the man.

She said he was there again last night.

She said that's when I called Betsy.

She said that will be all you need to know.

I said yes that wraps it up.

I said with this wealth of information I should have him on the gallows by dawn.

Candi Yakozi said I don't believe in capital punishment.

She said I don't believe in religion either.

She said or bullfighting.

She said what don't you believe in?

I shrugged.

I said just about everything.

I said what do you want me to do about the man?

She said just chase him away or something.

She gave me her address and her telephone number and seventy-five dollars.

She said can you start tonight?

I shrugged.

I said if I do I'll have to postpone a big blackmail case.

> *...only thing more confusing than a woman is two women....*
>
> MONROE D. UNDERWOOD

❖

It started raining about one o'clock.

I sat in the office and worked on a half-pint of Sunnybrook.

After Candi Yakozi I could have used a half-gallon.

I watched umbrellas blossom down on Dearborn Street.

I watched a Yellow Cab sideswipe a Checker Cab.

Later on I watched a Checker Cab sideswipe a Yellow Cab.

Vengeance is sweet.

I watched Winston on the window ledge.

I smoked a pack of cigarettes.

Betsy called at five o'clock.

She said how about my girl friend?

I said oh yes and by the way how about her?

Betsy said were you able to help her?

I said it is my professional opinion that Candi Yakozi is beyond help.

Betsy said I'm concerned about that man watching her.

I said don't worry about him.

I said he'll be all right if he doesn't strike up a conversation.

Betsy said have you been drinking?

I shrugged.

I said no more than necessary.

I said I'm going out there tonight.

Betsy said hold it.

She said let's get this straight.

She said what you are saying is that you are going to Candi Yakozi's place.

I said yes.

Betsy said and you are going to be in her apartment.

I shrugged.

I said probably.

I said is there something wrong with that?

Betsy groaned and the line went dead.

The rain stopped at dusk.

It was a steamy suffocating evening.

Neon signs were winking on as I drove north to Candi Yakozi's place.

The Blinking Dog.

Ye Olde Hades.

The Thirsty Knight.

The Gay Dragon.

Old Style and Budweiser and Pabst.

I popped my cassette of *Alte Kameraden* into the player.

A friend had taped it for me.

Alte Kameraden seven and one-half times.

The Royal Netherlands Guardsmen.

Music to enlist by.

It got my adrenaline moving.

By the time I reached Candi Yakozi's street I was ready to fight thirty-two Royal Bengal tigers.

38

I counted doorways from her address to the corner.

I parked and walked up the alley to the back door of her garden apartment.

I knocked lightly.

The door opened instantly.

Candi Yakozi was wearing a smile and spike heels and a white sharkskin blouse that came to a screeching halt something like fifteen inches north of her knees.

It looked like that might be all.

She took me into the living room.

She dropped onto a huge white sofa.

She locked her hands around her knees.

She drew them up to her chest.

She rocked back and forth slowly.

That was all by God.

I sat down.

I had to.

Candi said do you like my white blouse?

I shrugged.

I said it's fine as far as it goes.

Candi said I am very partial to white.

She said especially light white.

I said that's probably the best kind.

She had a cute little apartment.

All fluff and frills and white and pink.

Candi popped to her feet and went into the kitchen.

She had the lightning-quick grace of a kitten.

She came back with a cold bottle of beer.

She placed it in front of me.

She sat beside me on the sofa.

Very close.

She fired up a brace of cigarettes and handed one to me.

She said ooh I'm so glad you could get away from that nasty old blackmail case.

I said it wasn't easy kiddo.

I said I had to pull a few strings.

39

Candi said the man isn't out there yet.
I said let me know when he shows.
She said do you want some music?
I shrugged.
I said do you have a recording of *Alte Kameraden*?
Candi said I don't dig grand opera.
She got up and found some syrupy stuff on FM.
Faceless supermarket music.
She sat beside me again.
Much closer.
If possible.
She said I bet you meet an awful lot of girls.
I said some.
The small hand on my knee was soft and very warm.
Candi said do you take them to bed like the private detectives in the books?
I shrugged.
I said well not all at the same time.
I chuckled a nervous chuckle.
Candi said I bet you are just peachy in bed.
I said is he out there yet?
Candi cocked a venetian blind slat ever so slightly.
She said I don't see him.
I said well if he was out there you'd see him wouldn't you?
Candi said oh sure.
She said it's probably too early.
I said I wish he'd hurry.
Candi squeezed my leg.
She had a grip like a seven-hundred-dollar vise.
She said you didn't tell me.
I said I didn't tell you what?
She said how you are in bed.
I said you got another beer?
Candi whisked into the kitchen.
On her way back she paused to turn off one of her pink table lamps.

She put the beer down.
She sat beside me.
With her left leg over my right leg.
I said you could pull a hamstring muscle that way.
She said aren't you ever going to tell me?
I said just what was it you wanted to know?
Candi said my God for a private detective you sure got
a lousy memory.
I said is he out there yet?
Candi scrambled to her knees.
She looked over my shoulder through the aperture in
the venetian blind.
Her white sharkskin blouse caressed my jowl.
It made great rasping sounds.
Her perfume swept over me like a tidal wave.
My heart sounded like a washtub being beaten with a
leg of mutton.
Candi said not yet.
I said why that dirty bastard.
Sweat cascaded from my forehead.
I said Jesus Christ it's hot in here.
Candi said the thermostat is set at seventy-two.
I said you can't always trust them damn things.
Candi said Betsy told me you are simply wonderful in
bed.
I said yeah well maybe Betsy ain't such a good judge.
Candi said she ought to be.
She said Betsy's a whore.
I said call girl.
I said you're always supposed to say call girl.
Candi said Betsy told me you know just what to do for
a woman.
I said my God isn't that sonofabitch out there yet?
Candi turned out the other pink table lamp.
She looked through the venetian blind.
She said huh-uh.
I said how come you turned out the light to look?

My voice had risen about fourteen octaves.

Candi said so he can't see me looking.

I said how the hell can he see you looking if he isn't out there?

Candi said don't get all excited.

She said he'll get here.

I said I'm not all excited about him getting here.

I said I'm all excited about him getting here too goddam late.

The FM was playing "Help Me Make It Through the Night."

Candi put her head on my shoulder.

She hummed part of the bridge.

She said such a beautiful song.

She said it has great meaning.

She said it's so sexy.

She said what's your favorite song?

I shrugged.

I said *Alte Kameraden*.

I said also "The Teddy Bears' Picnic."

Candi said "The Teddy Bears' Picnic" can't be so very sexy.

I said that just shows how much you know about teddy bears.

Candi said are you sex-oriented?

I shrugged.

She said I am sex-oriented.

I said I was beginning to wonder about that.

I said you got another beer?

Candi said you haven't finished the first one yet.

I finished the first one.

I drank the second in three gulps.

I said I have this raging thirst.

I said it's probably just a relapse.

I said bubonic plague you know.

I said if he isn't out there I'm going looking for him.

Candi sighed.

She said I'm going to wear this damned blind out.
She looked.
She said well dammit all to hell anyway.
She said he's out there.

At the back door Candi Yakozi stood on tiptoes.
She bit my earlobe gently but with authority.
She whispered get this over with and hurry back to me.
On my way to the alley I fell over a bunch of garbage cans.
Twenty thousand dogs started barking.
A door flew open.
A big guy came out on a porch.
He had a flashlight that shone clear to Milwaukee.
Which is where I wished I was.
The big guy said what are you doing out there?
I said I am falling over a bunch of garbage cans.
He said what the hell do you want?
I said I want you to turn off that goddam flashlight.
I said you are putting me blind.
The big guy said I am going to call the cops.
I said where were you when I needed you?
He went in and slammed the door.

I hiked down to the end of the alley and up to the corner.

He was standing under a streetlight.

He was medium-sized.

He was smoking a cigarette.

I walked up to him.

He was a swarthy man with hot beady black eyes and a colossal hawklike nose.

A crooked white scar ran down his cheek and found sanctuary in a bristling walrus moustache.

He looked me over.

He blew smoke in my face.

He said hey whattsamatta you?

I said just what is your purpose in strolling up and down in front of that building on the other side of the street?

He said well inna firsta place amma notta strolla uppa downa fronta building other side street.

He said amma strolla uppa downa fronta building thissa side street.

He said hey if wanna strolla uppa downa fronta building other side street firsta thing do is crossa street.

He said thinka over onna way home.

He sneered.

He flipped his cigarette butt at me.

It hit my shoulder.

There was a shower of sparks.

He said okay kid?

I shrugged.

I brushed the ashes from my coat.

I said permit me to make a rather timely suggestion.

I said it is my rather timely suggestion that you get your ass out of this neighborhood before I kick it up around your ears.

He put his hand on his hips.

He spat on the sidewalk.

He said well amma greaseaballa sonnabitch.

I said that's the most sense you've made so far.

He gave no warning.

He just cut loose with a whistling haymaker.

I ducked.

I could hear a car approaching.

He swung again.

This time he came close.

I pawed at him with my left.

I heard the car squeal to a stop.

He had circled away from me.

My back was to the street.

He smiled knowingly.

I heard the car door slam.

He had help on the way.

I landed an overhand right that drove him into a big clump of Japanese yews next door.

Somebody grabbed my shoulder.

I spun free.

I blasted the new guy with a roundhouse left that draped him over the hood of his car.

It was a big black car.

Like in the gangster movies.

The cops came.

> ... oncet upon a time there was a woman
> what took no for a answer ... they stuffed
> her and put her in a museum. ...
>
> MONROE D. UNDERWOOD

At the Shakespeare police station a grizzled old desk
sergeant was gargling a salami sandwich and working on
a crossword puzzle.

Kellis J. Ammson was cupping a hand to his swollen
jaw.

He was pointing a shaking finger in my direction.

He said I want this man electrocuted and deported to
flaming Transylvania.

I shrugged.

I said how was I to know he was working for you?

The station door flew open.

Candi Yakozi swept into the room.

She embraced me.

Passionately.

She kissed me.

Lingeringly.

She looked into my eyes.

Worshipfully.

She said you are my hero.
She said love me and the world is mine.
I shrugged.
I said the guy's name is Gino Scarletti.
I said he is a private eye from the Ammson agency.
I said your husband was having you watched.
She said where is my husband?
I said New Hampshire.
Candi Yakozi nodded.
She said I knew it was somewhere around there.
Gino Scarletti kept flexing his jaw and blinking.
He said hola worlda screwed up.
Kellis J. Ammson said I know it Gino.
He said but it was okay until Purdue came along.
The grizzled old desk sergeant looked up from his crossword puzzle.
He said private detectives give me a royal screaming pain in the ass.
He said I will now give the whole bunch of you just thirty seconds to clear the goddam premises.
Kellis J. Ammson trumpeted like a teed-off bull elephant.
He said this flaming homicidal mental case attacks two law-abiding citizens and you just sit there with a flaming coloring book.
The grizzled old desk sergeant said this is a crossword-puzzle book you imbecile.
He said you now got fifteen seconds.
On the way out Kellis J. Ammson glared at Candi Yakozi.
He said oh boy is your flaming husband ever going to get a report on you you flaming whore.
Candi Yakozi snarled.
She said call girl you uncouth boor.
She took me by the arm.
She said what is an uncouth boor?
She said I heard it on TV.

She snuggled up to me.
She said you are coming home with me.
I shrugged.
I was too tired to say no.

The next morning Betsy was in my office at nine-forty-five.

I stuffed my copy of *Eagles* magazine into a drawer.

I said you're early kiddo.

Betsy didn't reply.

Her face was expressionless.

She handed me a container of steaming black coffee.

She gave me a cigarette.

She held her lighter for me.

She stroked my head.

She gave me a pat on the cheek.

She said sweetheart angel apple-dumpling love of my life.

I said speak sweetlips.

She said Chance I am going to kill you you sonofabitch so help me Christ.

I said your girl friend damn near beat you to it.

I said I had to play *Alte Kameraden* all the way to the office.

Betsy's pale blue eyes were blazing.

She said why you lying cheating philandering casanova romeo gigolo any old port in a storm man about town.

I said who's lying?

Betsy said Candi Yakozi called me right after you left.

She said that female was absolutely delirious.

I said is that unusual?

Betsy said Candi Yakozi thinks you are the greatest thing since popcorn.

I said that figures.

I said she sure buttered me up.

Betsy said who seduced whom?

I shrugged.

I said I have no idea.

Betsy said how incredibly odd.

She said first you lose your self-control and now you have misplaced your memory.

She said I hope you still have your socks.

I said do not jest.

I said it was a traumatic experience.

I said I may never be the same.

Betsy said spare me the sordid details.

I said doesn't that Candi Yakozi ever sleep?

Betsy went to the door.

She said after I pick up some uniforms I'll take you to lunch.

She said permit me to recommend the *Strychnine au Cyanide*.

I said uniforms?

Betsy said black underwear Beau Philo.
She said I'm a working girl.
She went out.
She nearly took the door off its hinges.

After the steak sandwich I was nipping on my green chartreuse and sipping on my coffee.

I said is Candi Yakozi a whore?

Betsy said now say it right.

I said is she a call girl?

Betsy said of course.

She said Candi just might make some money if she'd stop giving it away.

Betsy poked at the brandy ice with her spoon.

She was staring at me.

She said you bum.

I said how long can a woman be a call girl?

Betsy said as long as she wants to I guess.

I said what happens when she gets old?

Betsy said well instead of being a young call girl she is an old call girl.

I said how long do you figure to be a call girl?

Betsy said until you marry me.

I said boy I sure hate to think of you being an old call
girl.
Betsy said not a chance.
She said I'll get you before then.
I said do you enjoy your work?
Betsy frowned.
She said oh some of it is very good.
She said some of it is very bad.
She said most of it is very ho-hum.
She said but it keeps me from missing you.
She said which reminds me.
She said it's been almost forever.
I shrugged.
I said we'll go to my place next time.
Betsy said but I have a water mattress.
I said you also got a goddam phone.
I reached for the check.
Betsy beat me to the draw.
I didn't argue.

...other day they caught a feller what wasn't overthrowing the govinment... wasn't demonstrating ... wasn't queer ... wasn't practicing no yoga ... wasn't bothering nobody ... wasn't doing nothing but going to work every day ... throwed him in the loony bin ... said he had no place in today's advanced society....

MONROE D. UNDERWOOD

That afternoon a little guy with straggly red hair and shiny blue eyes came in.

He said I want you to find out why my mother is receiving a lot of obscene telephone calls.

I said well before we find out why we got to find out who.

He said oh that's easy.

He said I know who.

I said who?

He said me.

He said but I don't know why.

I sent him over the Ammson Private Detective Agency.

I said Ammson is absolutely tops in situations of this nature.

❈

I was reading the last page of "Revenge Flies a Silver
Spad" when the telephone rang.

It was a gruff-voiced man who told me his name was
D. L. Ambercrombie.

He said D. L. Ambercrombie of Ambercrombie and
Jones.

I said oh yes.

I said the exterminators.

Ambercrombie said no you are thinking of Abrams and
Brown.

He said you were recommended by one of your recent
clients.

He said can you come up to Logan Square about four
o'clock this afternoon?

He said it's most important.

I said just a moment.

I said one of my secretaries is out on an errand.

I said I think the other one is in the can.

57

I said let me check the appointment book.
I finished "Revenge Flies a Silver Spad."
I put the *Eagles* magazine away.
I picked up the phone.
I said Mr. Ambercrombie it looks like you're in luck.
I said how's four-thirty?
I said I'll try to make it earlier but I'm all tied up on a big embezzlement case.
Ambercrombie said I understand.
He said four-thirty will be fine.
He gave me the address.
He said be careful.
He said this is very hush-hush.
He said don't talk to anybody but Myrtle Culpepper.
He said she's my receptionist and she'll show you right in.

> *. . . some women is less amazing than others . . . I ain't never met none of them kind. . . .*

�

Ambercrombie and Jones was an agency for Northern Consolidated Insurance.

The ordinary store-front property was beautifully done inside.

It was paneled in black walnut.

It had vertical venetian blinds and ankle-deep salt-and-pepper carpeting and oil paintings and soft lighting.

It had rubber trees and ivy plants.

It had FM music.

And it had Myrtle Culpepper.

Myrtle Culpepper was a dead ringer for Whistler's mother.

Only she was older.

She wore a navy blue high-collared dress with a little gold World War I service pin at the throat.

Her faded lips smiled a welcome.

Her voice was no more than slightly cracked.

She said Mr. Purdue?

I took off my hat and held it like when they play "The Star-Spangled Banner."

I said yes ma'am.

Myrtle Culpepper's eyelashes fluttered like little lost butterflies.

She said Mr. Purdue permit me to compliment you on your excellent manners and on your haircut.

She said these days one meets so very few genuine gentlemen with masculine haircuts.

I shrugged.

I blushed.

I said yes ma'am.

Myrtle Culpepper giggled.

She said oh heavens how utterly sweet.

She put a waxen hand to bluish hair.

She nodded toward the rear of the building.

She said Mr. Ambercrombie is expecting you.

There were two doors.

One was orange and open.

It had D. L. AMBERCROMBIE on it in white plastic letters.

The other door was beige and closed.

It had no name on it.

I figured the nameless door belonged to Jones.

If your name is Jones why bother?

Not that Jones isn't a hell of a name.

Some of my best friends are Joneses.

D. L. Ambercrombie was slouched in a high-backed executive chair.

He was a short burly man.

He reminded me of a gray-haired fireplug.

He looked vaguely familiar.

He had a foot up on the corner of his desk.

There was a hole in the heel of his sock.

I like men with holes in their socks.

Their unimpressiveness impresses me.

Ambercrombie waved hello.

He said sit down Purdue.

He said I got your name from a Miss Yakozi earlier in the day.

He said she mentioned that you handled a personal matter for her last night.

He said Miss Yakozi told me that you acted most expeditiously.

Ambercrombie brought his foot from the desk to the floor with a bang.

He said Purdue this is no assignment for a dummy.

He said I want an intelligent man of action.

I shrugged.

I said the action part comes real easy.

Ambercrombie grinned apologetically.

He said well you know what I mean.

He said some private detectives are dummies.

He lowered his voice.

He said can we speak man to man?

I said I guess we got to.

I said there ain't nobody else here.

Ambercrombie said I know a lady who hired a dummy private detective to follow her husband.

He said only a couple days ago when I was doing some collecting for a sick agent.

He said would you believe that this dummy detective followed me around for hours?

I said I just bet that this dummy detective thought he was tailing her husband.

Ambercrombie laughed uproariously.

He said he had to give her money back.

He said he sure was a dummy.

I said you better get your taillight fixed.

Ambercrombie stared at me.

I said I think maybe I am clairvoyant.

Ambercrombie said well by God.

I said how well do you know Miss Yakozi?

Ambercrombie winked.

He said about three hundred dollars' worth.

He said how about you?

I said somewhere between not well enough and to
goddam well.

Ambercrombie said I ought to get Jones in here.

He said but he has a couple of guys in his office.

He said Jones and I have been in business for thirt
years and we've never seen anything like this.

He said three Friday mornings ago six hundred dolla
was missing from our safe.

He said two Friday mornings ago we were minus seve
hundred.

He said last Friday it was eight hundred.

Ambercrombie scowled.

He said you know what I think?

I said sure.

I said you think it will be nine hundred this Friday.

Ambercrombie said I think some sonofabitch is stealin
money.

I said you probably got something there.

Ambercrombie said this is Thursday.

He said can you spend tonight here and find out wha
is happening?

It was a quick arrangement.

Ambercrombie gave me seventy-five dollars and a ke
to the office.

He scribbled his home telephone number on the bac
of a business card.

He said call me if anything happens.

I said I'll do better than that.

I said I'll call you even if nothing happens.

Ambercrombie nodded approvingly.

He said you're a damn good man Purdue.

�֎

I walked west on Diversey Avenue to Booligan's Bar.
It was a blistering block.
It took four bottles of beer to cool me off.
Booligan wasn't on duty.
I asked about him.
The new bartender told me Booligan was at the Ravenswood Hospital.
I said who's sick?
The new bartender looked surprised at my question.
He said Booligan.
He said didn't you hear about the rape case?
I said no.
He said some elderly lady.
I said good Christ don't tell me Booligan raped some elderly lady.
The new bartender said don't worry I won't.
He said some elderly lady raped Booligan.
I said impossible.

The new bartender said well maybe you ought to run right over to Ravenswood Hospital and explain that to Booligan.

He said I am sure he will be very pleased to hear it.

He said the old gal nailed him while he was turning out the lights.

He shook his head.

He said she really did a job on him.

He said very professional.

He said you ever been raped?

I said I'm not sure.

❀

I waited until dark.

I walked back to my car and got my brand-new three-cell flashlight.

I let myself into the Ambercrombie and Jones offices.

I checked the safe in Ambercrombie's office.

It was locked.

I sat at Myrtle Culpepper's desk.

Under the desk glass were a few pictures of a couple in the fifties.

There were several of younger couples.

Their ages ranged from twenty-five to thirty-five.

There were about a dozen of kids anywhere from five to fifteen.

I chuckled.

Myrtle Culpepper was a great-grandmother.

Great-grandmothers were the backbone of the nation.

God bless all great-grandmothers.

I turned off my brand-new three-cell flashlight.

I just sat there.
There is nothing worse than just sitting there.
I wished I had brought a six-pack.
In about an hour I changed my mind.
I wished I had brought a twelve-pack.
I tried to call Betsy.
No answer.
I looked around for the FM set.
When I found it I decided not to turn it on.
You just almost never hear *Alte Kameraden* on FM.
I went back to Myrtle Culpepper's desk.
I tried to call Betsy.
No answer.

...oncet I knowed a feller what was tic-tac-toe champion of Bannerville Georgia ...they got him in the Tic-Tac-Toe Hall of Fame....

MONROE D. UNDERWOOD

✖

By ten o'clock I had burned almost a pack of cigarettes.
The place was pitch black.
The air-conditioning was off.
It was hotter than hell in there.
I was sorry I hadn't brought a copy of *Eagles* magazine.
I could have read it with my brand-new three-cell flashlight.
I played tic-tac-toe in my mind.
I had the x's.
Playing tic-tac-toe in your mind is extremely difficult.
Especially in the dark.
I kept making round x's.
I lost damn near every game.
I tried to call Betsy.
Still no answer.

About midnight I was beginning to doze.

Then I heard a key hit the lock.

I dropped behind Myrtle Culpepper's desk.

The door opened.

Somebody whispered amma go inna finda safe.

Somebody else whispered I'll check the back and I'll be right with you.

A flashlight clicked on.

Somebody passed Myrtle Culpepper's desk.

I stood up.

I hit him on top of the head with my brand-new three-cell flashlight.

He sagged silently into the thick salt-and-pepper carpeting.

I turned off his flashlight.

I stood beside the door and waited.

In a few seconds somebody else came in.

68

I hit him on top of the head with my brand-new three-cell flashlight.

He collapsed face down.

I went to Myrtle Culpepper's desk and grabbed the telephone.

I called D. L. Ambercrombie.

He answered on the first ring.

He said Purdue?

I said you ain't just a-woofing.

He said what's up?

I said grab some cops and get over here.

I said it's all history.

D. L. Ambercrombie said I could tell you were a damn good man.

*...when you meet some people twicet
that's oncet too often....*

MONROE D. UNDERWOOD

At the Shakespeare police station Kellis J. Ammson was
holding his head with both hands.

He was talking to the grizzled old desk sergeant.

He said officer society must deal sternly with this man.

He said he goes around braining people with flaming
three-cell flashlights.

He said he is undoubtedly the greatest flaming menace
since Attila the Hun.

He said and I am not so flaming sure about Attila the
Hun.

I shrugged.

I said I didn't know Jones had hired you guys.

Ambercrombie said that's right officer.

He said even I didn't know.

He said while I was hiring this guy Jones was hiring
these guys.

Gino Scarletti said oh Jeeza Christ I think I onna
wronga side.

70

I said I wrecked my brand-new three-cell flashlight.
The grizzled old desk sergeant leaned back in his chair.
His faded eyes gleamed strangely.
He clawed at the gray stubble on his chin.
He said well they told me vaudeville was coming back.
He said I was a fool.
He said I wouldn't believe.
He said but here it is by God.
He said you fellas got one hell of an act.
He said but I ain't much on encores.
He said get out of my goddam police station.

...you sleep with one woman you sleep with them all ... feller what found that out sure didn't allow much time for drinking....

MONROE D. UNDERWOOD

I stopped at a tavern.
I had a double Jack Daniels.
I tried to call Betsy.
No answer.
I had a double Jack Daniels.
I tried to call Betsy.
No answer.
I had a double Jack Daniels.
The bartender said we're closing up pal.
I called Candi Yakozi.
Candi Yakozi said I recommended you to my insurance man.
I said I think maybe we better talk about that.
She said okay come right over.
She said this afternoon I bought a recording of *Alte Kameraden*.
She said it's a terrific polka.
She said I couldn't find "The Teddy Bears' Picnic."

I said do you have any patriotic music?
I said I'm proud to be an American.
Candi said I got "Columbia the Gem of the Ocean."
I said who does it?
She said I think it is the Mormon Tabernacle Choir.
She said but it might be Elvis Presley.
She said what's the difference?
I said you got beer?
Candi said I got a refrigerator full.
She said I'm proud to be an American too.
I said have you ever heard "Hats Off the Flag Is Passing
By"?
She said no but I'd love to.
I shrugged.
I said leave a light on.

�֎

I had been in the office less than an hour when Booligan came limping in.

Booligan was missing some hair.

His face was scratched.

His lower lip was swollen.

He said I got a job for you.

He said I want you to find the old broad who raped me.

I said hey was she that good?

Booligan said I bet you are a real riot at a funeral.

I said I was going to send you a card.

I said one with lilies and things.

Booligan said cards wouldn't help none.

I said how come you didn't fight her off?

Booligan used a four-letter word.

He said you ever fight a she-grizzly bear?

He said from now on I am keeping a sawed-off shotgun behind the bar.

He said and a fifty-gallon drum of Mace.

74

He said that old broad scares me to death.

I said maybe she wanted money.

Booligan said money hell.

He said she left me forty dollars.

He said she was lugging a roll that would of choked a hippopotamus.

He said she's a sex maniac.

He said she's dangerous.

I said don't sweat it.

I said the cops have to catch up with her sooner or later.

Booligan said sooner or later ain't soon enough.

He said you know Spud?

I said from Spud's Place?

Booligan nodded.

He said she raped Spud last night.

He said she left Spud twenty-five dollars.

He said Spud is in a state of shock.

I said well that just got to be a big improvement.

I said are you sure it's the same broad?

Booligan said who else?

He said how many old broads go around raping bartenders?

I said well offhand I would say less than fifty percent.

Booligan dropped a hundred-dollar bill on my desk.

He said start looking.

He said this goddam Women's Lib thing is getting out of hand.

He hobbled out cussing a bright blue streak.

*... I got to give whores credit ... wisht I
could find one what would do likewise. ...*

MONROE D. UNDERWOOD

�

After Booligan left I got a call from D. L. Ambercrombie.

He said goddam sonofabitching goddam sonofabitching goddam sonofabitch.

I said what's wrong?

D. L. Ambercrombie said you were right that's what's wrong.

He said this morning it was nine hundred dollars.

He said but this time it's marked money.

He said yesterday I put a red moustache on the picture of every sonofabitch in the goddam safe.

Betsy came in.

I told Ambercrombie I'd be getting back to him.

He said you're a damn good man Purdue.

Betsy sat in the client's chair.

She didn't dust it off.

She leaned back.

She didn't cross her legs.

76

Her soft mouth was a hard crimson gash.

Her pale blue eyes glittered like Kellis J. Ammson's diamonds.

She said so see Chance Purdue.

She said see Chance Purdue spend two straight nights with Candi Yakozi.

She said see Betsy.

She said see Betsy boil Candi Yakozi in oil.

I chuckled good-naturedly.

She said see Betsy castrate Chance Purdue.

I said now you just wait a goddam minute Betsy.

Betsy stood up.

She said oh well.

She said all's fair in love and war.

She leaned over and kissed my cheek.

She winked at me.

She smiled.

It was a strange distant smile.

She went out.

She didn't mention lunch.

On the window ledge Winston looked puzzled.

> *...sure I served my country...allus got Taps mixed up with Mess Call...got throwed out of more goddam mess halls....*
>
> MONROE D. UNDERWOOD

�֍

That afternoon a large man with an iron-gray crew cut marched in.

He was wearing a conservative charcoal suit.

He had flinty blue eyes and a jutting jaw.

There was something about him that said no nonsense.

He said Mr. Purdue my name is Clem Dawson.

He gave me a firm handshake.

He said I am with the United States government.

I said you must be very lonely.

Dawson settled into the client's chair.

He said I mean I work for the government.

He whipped a calfskin folder from an inside pocket.

He flashed enough identification to get him into the President's liquor cabinet.

He said Purdue we know all about you.

I said oh my God.

Dawson said if there is anything you wish to know about yourself please feel free to ask.

78

I said what's my middle name?

Dawson didn't blink.

He said you don't have a middle name.

I shrugged.

I said okay.

Dawson leaned forward in the client's chair.

He had a crisp to-the-point manner of speaking.

He said Purdue the United States government has a proposition for you.

I said now that makes two.

I said the first one didn't pan out too well.

Dawson nodded.

He said well the infantryman always ends up on the wrong end of the shaft.

I said I was in the field artillery.

Dawson said field artillery supports infantry.

He said you didn't earn your Bronze Star three miles behind the lines.

He said you were up front with that radio.

I shrugged.

I said I should have got the Congressional Medal of Honor just for carrying the goddam thing.

I said it was bigger than me.

I said what's the proposition?

Dawson said three hundred dollars per week for occasional investigatory work.

I said that's the only kind of investigatory work I do.

I said is it dangerous?

Dawson said this depends on just how good you are.

I said that could make it pretty goddam dangerous.

Dawson lit a cork-tipped cigarette with an ancient Zippo.

I said how long does this job figure to last?

Dawson frowned.

He said the end is nowhere in sight.

I said at that rate I might be able to pay off my car.

Dawson lowered his voice.

He said Purdue have you ever heard of DADA?

I shrugged.

I said not since I was very young.

Dawson said DADA stands for Destroy America Destroy America.

I whistled.

I said they must mean it.

I said they said it twice.

Dawson's jutting jaw hardened.

He said you had better believe they mean it.

He said DADA is a highly efficient subversive organization founded and funded by the Kremlin.

He said its original assignment was to acquire complete control of the news media of this country.

He said of course that mission was accomplished many years ago.

He said since then DADA has been a sort of jack-of-all-trades machine.

He said it has dabbled in everything from campus agitation to cold-blooded murder.

He said we have good reason to believe that DADA was responsible for the student riots at Purity State Theological Seminary in Phoebus Virginia.

He said there is little doubt that DADA blew up the Happy Giant Ice Cream plant in Lickdale Pennsylvania.

I said this DADA really gets around.

Dawson smiled wryly.

He said now we have it on excellent authority that DADA is gearing up for a new operation of major proportions.

I said who is Mr. Big?

Dawson sighed.

He said our best sources indicate that DADA is headed by a Nivlek Ysteb.

Dawson pronounced it Ee-steb.

He said he is probably of Belgian extraction.

He said there is an Ysteb River in Belgium.

I said boy he must be good if they named a river after him.

Dawson cleared his throat noisily.

He said Nivlek Ysteb is a shadowy figure at best.

He said we have no dossier and no description and no leads.

He said in short Purdue we have us a major-league headache.

He said national security is undoubtedly at stake.

I said is DADA in Chicago?

Dawson gave a short humorless laugh.

He said DADA is everywhere.

He said we are theorizing that Chicago is its headquarters.

I said why don't you bring in the FBI or the CIA?

Dawson shook his head sadly.

He said by the time our DADA-controlled news media gets through there won't be an FBI or CIA.

I said I'm beginning to get the picture.

I said hell there may not even be a PTA.

I said but why me?

Dawson looked me squarely in the eye.

He said Purdue you're our best bet.

He said you're a patriotic cuss.

He said you work alone.

He said you move quickly and you're experienced and tough.

He said you're resourceful and you're capable of positive action.

He said you're our man right down the line.

He said providing you can meet a couple of conditions.

I said for twelve hundred a month I'm listening.

Dawson said well for openers you'll have to close this office.

I said what happens to all my clients?

Dawson brushed a fleck of cigarette ash from his coat sleeve.

He said by God Purdue there's a sparrow on your window ledge.

I said that's Winston.

I said what about my lease?

Dawson dismissed the lease with a curt wave of his hand.

He said we'll take care of the minor matters.

I said what's the other condition?

Dawson rubbed the side of his nose.

He said I'm afraid it may strike you as being a trifle odd.

I said hey you should hear some of the goofy offers I get.

I said just the other day a guy came in here with an idea.

I said he told me if I would hold up the Dearborn Trust and Savings he would split the money with me.

Dawson said what did you tell him?

I said I told him I don't have a gun.

Dawson said don't you?

I said of course not.

I said if I had a gun I might shoot somebody.

I said probably me.

Dawson licked his lips.

He said go on with the story.

I said well this guy offered to loan me his bow and arrow.

I said I sent him over to the Ammson Private Detective Agency.

Dawson said naturally your ingenuity weighed most heavily in our selection.

He took a deep breath and exhaled loudly.

In a little while he said okay Purdue here it comes.

He said we want you to move in with your lady friend.

The only sound in the office was the ticking of my wristwatch.

It was deafening.

I said move in with who?

Dawson said don't scream like that.

He said the young lady on Kelvin Avenue.

He said that fetching little blonde on the second floor.

He said the one you didn't have lunch with today.

I thought about it.

I said it is sure as hell a small world.

I said do you know there is just a chance that you are talking about Betsy?

I stood up.

I said well Mr. Dawson it has been simply divine but you must excuse me.

I said I am terribly overdue on something like forty murder cases.

I said not to mention any number of kidnappings.

I said besides I am going to hold up the Dearborn Trust and Savings.

Dawson motioned for me to sit down.

He said Purdue believe me this is the only way it will work.

I said great God man there must be a better way than that.

I said why you are killing the dog to get rid of the fleas.

I said you are feeding the cat to the goddam mice.

I said you are cutting down the goddam trees so you can see the goddam forest.

Dawson's face had turned brick red.

He banged my desk with his fist.

He said cool it Purdue.

He said this is no goddam time to go into hysterics.

He said now you listen to me.

He said can't you see that a man shouldn't go around investigating a crackerjack Soviet organization while operating out of a downtown office?

He said why DADA might blow up the goddam building.

I said well that's a lot better than getting Betsy's apartment blown up.

I said Betsy got a nice apartment.

I said she just put up new drapes.

Dawson said Purdue will you stop waving your arms and sit down and shut up?

Winston was fluttering wildly on the window ledge.

Dawson said do it our way and DADA will never suspect.

He said you merely have to pretend that you weren't doing too well on your own.

I said a man hates to live a lie.

Dawson said we just want you to look domesticated.

He said low profile all the way.

I said do you know what you're asking?

I said do you know what happens to me if I move in with Betsy?

I said I never get out that's what happens to me.

I said why don't you move in with Betsy?

Dawson didn't reply.

He just sat there looking forlorn.

Finally he said Purdue please sit down.

I sat down.

I said well you see how it is.

Dawson looked up.

His eyes were moist.

His voice quavered.

He said this is for your country Purdue.

I said for Christ's sake Dawson she's a whore.

Dawson said isn't call girl more appropriate?

I said but that goddam telephone.

Dawson placed a white card on the corner of my desk.

He said this is the combination for an Elmwood Park Post Office box.

He said you will pick up your pay and instructions there each Friday.

He said you may also leave word regarding your progress.

I shrugged.

I said breathes there the man with soul so dead.

Dawson had pulled out a big blue bandanna.

He dabbed at his eyes.

He said God bless you Purdue.
He said America needs more men of your caliber.
He gave me a pat on the shoulder.
He went out.
He closed the door softly behind him.
Like they do in hospitals.
And funeral parlors.
I shrugged.
I dug a half-pint of Sunnybrook out of a desk drawer.
Well what the hell.
We all got to go sometime.

*. . . onliest trouble with great patriots is we
ain't got none. . . .*

MONROE D. UNDERWOOD

❈

It was eleven peeyem at Wallace's.
The Sox had just finished losing to Cleveland 10-1.
I had just wiped out my ninth beer.
One per inning.
I am very good at arithmetic.
Wallace turned off the television set.
He brought me a beer.
Wallace was a big guy.
He was sixty or so.
He had faded red hair.
What there was of it.
He had a sagging belly and saddle-brown eyes and no
teeth and flat feet and a perpetual hangover and an ex-
cellent business.
Wallace operated the average-guy sort of gin mill.
Twenty stools and six booths.

No pool table.

No pinball machines.

Friendly middle-aged neighborhood traffic.

When the ball game went off so did the television.

Wallace detested soap operas and quiz shows.

He couldn't tolerate situation comedies and police stuff.

Old movies bored him and new ones disturbed him.

Commercials drove him crazy.

Wallace's opinion of television was wrapped up in one nasty little word.

Wallace put his elbows on the bar.

He sighed.

He said I am going to sell this firetrap and move to Georgia.

He said I am going to buy a cotton gin.

He said I keep getting these awful Chicago headaches.

He said it's the air pollution and them Sox.

He said them Sox is destroying me.

Old Dad Underwood spoke up.

Speaking up was Old Dad Underwood's greatest fault.

He said them Sox is only a couple years away.

Wallace said from what?

Old Dad Underwood said well right about now it looks like bankruptcy.

Wallace looked at me.

He shook his head.

He said if your girl friend wasn't coming through the door I'd kill him on the spot.

Betsy approached with her slightly pigeon-toed panther walk.

She popped onto the stool next to mine.

She said hi Philo.

She winked at Wallace.

Wallace blushed and spilled a glass of beer.

Betsy fished a pack of Kools out of a handbag almost the size of a medicine ball.

She lit up and blew a few smoke rings.

One inside the other.

Betsy is very good at smoke rings.

She said I was in the neighborhood.

I said you still are.

Betsy said so what's happening?

I shrugged.

I said oh not a hell of a lot.

I said except I am going to move in with you.

Betsy turned slowly on her barstool.

She gave me a very sober look.

She said Chance let us not go around making jokes about matters that are not matters to go around making jokes about.

I said it's true.

I said I got to live with you for awhile.

I said it has to do with a big investigation I am conducting.

I said it is top-drawer stuff.

I said living with you will be sort of a cover.

I said nothing more than that you understand.

Betsy said oh?

She put her cigarette out.

She lit another.

She was trembling just a bit.

She said now Philo I have tidings for you.

She said big investigation or no big investigation there is one thing you damn well better know before you move in with me.

I said never mind.

I said I already know.

I said I'll never get out.

Betsy said my love you may go to the head of the class.

I shrugged.

I finished my beer.

I ordered a shot of Sunnybrook.

I drank a toast to freedom.

I ordered another and drank a toast to my country.

Then I toasted George Washington and General Black Jack Pershing and Franklin Delano Roosevelt and Stonewall Jackson.

I toasted Dick Tracy and Babe Ruth and Ulysses S. Grant and Bela Lugosi.

Not necessarily in that order.

I toasted Horatio Alger and John Dillinger.

I said gimme another drink.

I said I think I forgot Ethan Allen.

Betsy called Wallace over.

She said had he been drinking when he got here?

Wallace nodded.

Betsy said and how many have you served him?

Wallace said well if he gets one for Ethan Allen it will be maybe twenty.

Betsy said oh-oh.

She said we got big trouble.

She said that much always shifts him into a patriotic gear.

I said let's have one for good old Ethan Allen.

Betsy said I have to get him home somehow.

She said time is of the essence.

She said he's about due to give us The Pledge of Allegiance.

She said have you ever heard him do "Hats Off the Flag Is Passing By"?

Wallace blanched.

I said how about one for Ethan Allen?

Wallace said I better have Old Dad Underwood watch the joint.

He said I'll drive over to your place and give you a hand.

Betsy said surely goodness and mercy will follow you all the days of your life.

I said just one more for Ethan Allen.

They stuffed me into Betsy's car.

I said Ethan Allen isn't going to like this.

Betsy got in and started the engine.

I said hold it.

I said this operation is hereby declared suspended.

I said what about my automobile?

Betsy said we'll get it later.

I said my *Alte Kameraden* tape is in there.

Betsy said stick your head out of the window.

She said you don't look well.

I said be not deceived.

I said I am at the top of my game.

On the way to Betsy's I sang "America the Beautiful."

Several times.

Betsy said Chance it's spacious skies not skacious pie.

I said Betsy who is singing this song me or you?

Wallace and Betsy dragged me up the stairs.

I said I regret that I have but one life to give for my country.

I said shoot if you must this old gray head but spare your country's flag you rotten bastards.

I said Lafayette we are here so get your blooming ass in gear.

I said damn the torpedoes full speed ahead.

They dumped me onto the bed.

Wallace said he's really gung ho tonight.

Betsy said what did I tell you?

She said next comes the close-order drill business.

She said hut two three four to the rear march hut two three four.

She said like that.

Wallace said my God.

He said can you get his clothes off?

Betsy said thus far it has never presented a particularly difficult problem.

Wallace said good-night.

I said hut two three four.

I said unfettered I shall rise and fly into the freedom
of blue sky.*

Betsy said don't you bet on it baby.

> And there on eager pinion soar
> O'er cloud and rainbow evermore;
> With Rising Sun to light my way
> I'll bomb Pearl Harbor twice a day.

I woke up somewhere around noon.

I had the granddaddy of all the headaches in history.

Betsy was hanging my blue sports coat in the closet.

I said I thought I was wearing my brown sports coat.

Betsy said you were.

I said but that is my blue sports coat.

I said I believe an explanation is in order.

Betsy said I took your keys and picked up your clothing.

She said Wallace will bring the rest of your things this afternoon.

She said including your wallet and the shoe you left in his tavern.

I said he better be careful with my recording of *Alte Kameraden*.

I said recordings of *Alte Kameraden* don't grow on trees.

I said I hope you didn't lose anything.

92

Betsy said nothing but a little black book.
I groaned.
I said how did that happen?
Betsy said it fell into the toilet.
I said by accident of course.
Betsy said of course.
I said and then somebody flushed the toilet.
Betsy said how did you know that?
I said I'm a detective.
Betsy said would you believe it took four times to make
  those little pieces go down?
I said where the hell is my automobile?
Betsy said it's right in front of the building.
I said let me guess what building.
I said the Wrigley Building.
Betsy said Chance your car is right here.
She said you can see it from the window.
I said how did you bring that off?
Betsy said I took a cab to your car.
She said can you figure it from there?
I said you are a diabolically clever female.
Betsy said oh sweetheart if you only knew.
I said is there a sparrow on the window ledge?
Betsy said yes.
I said that's Winston.
I went back to sleep.

> *...only govinment man I ever knowed was a meat inspector...got hoof and mouth disease...they had to shoot him....*
>
> MONROE D. UNDERWOOD

On Friday morning I drove to the Elmwood Park Post Office.

There was an envelope in the box.

It contained six crisp fifty-dollar bills.

Typewritten on a small white card was FIND NIVLE YSTEB.

*. . . living with a woman ain't so bad pro-
viding a man don't make a habit of it. . . .*

MONROE D. UNDERWOOD

※

I drove back to Betsy's place.
The moment I stepped out of my car Mary Bright's
airedale broke loose.
I had to go all out to beat him to the door by a length.
Bonzo reared up on the glass.
His eyes were shining.
His tongue was hanging out.
He smiled at me.
So did Mary Bright.
I waved to Mary Bright.
She waved back.
Bonzo barked.
I went upstairs.
Betsy had left a note.
She was out on a call.
I sprawled on the couch and read a story in *Eagles*
magazine.
"Death Birds of the Argonne Skies."

After that I played a game of chess with myself.
Stalemate.
I watched part of the ball game on television.
The Cubs were getting massacred.
I ate a ham sandwich with horseradish mustard.
I drank two cans of beer.
It was very hot horseradish mustard.
I found my recording of *Alte Kameraden*.
It sounded great on Betsy's big set.
I smoked a pack of cigarettes.
I fell asleep on the couch.
It had been an afternoon of utter debauchery.

Betsy woke me up about five o'clock.

I said that was one hell of a long call.

Betsy said those were three very short calls.

I said is that better?

Betsy said it isn't better but it pays a hundred dollars
more.

I said I guess that's better.

Betsy said I guess.

She went into the kitchen and I could hear her bustling
around.

She whistled "Get Me to the Church on Time."

I was watching the six o'clock news when she called
me in.

There was steak and mushrooms and sliced tomatoes
and chocolate pudding topped with whipped cream and
a maraschino cherry.

Betsy is a good cook.

That night we played cribbage.

It is hard to find a woman who can play cribbage.

Betsy is very good at cribbage.

Betsy beat my brains out.

Six straight.

She skunked me three times.

She apologized.

She said sweetie there really isn't much skill in cribbage.

She said I just kept drawing those double runs.

I said I noticed that.

Betsy said you'll win next time.

I said that's the same old crock they kept handing Napoleon.

Betsy made coffee and we drank it at the kitchen table by candlelight.

Betsy makes excellent coffee.

After a long silence Betsy said you seem a bit down in the mouth tonight.

I said it must have been that afternoon nap.

Betsy said good Lord Chance are you jealous of what I do?

I shrugged.

I said I don't know.

I said well maybe.

I said but just a little bit.

Betsy said you don't know how happy that makes me.

She said but you shouldn't be jealous.

She said you've known for more than three years.

I said sure but I've only lived with you for a few days.

Betsy said aw Chance.

She reached across the table and squeezed my chin.

She was smiling but there were tears on her cheeks.

In the candlelight they looked like gold.

I brushed them away.

Betsy said honey do you remember the first time?

She said you got my number and you called me.

She said I came for an hour and I spent the night and I wouldn't take your money.

She said boy were you ever something special.
She said I've loved you ever since.
She said I just can't help it.
I said so what the hell are you crying about?
Betsy gave me a sniffling little grin.
She said you would never understand.
She said for God's sake come to bed.
I said who says there ain't no mental telepathy?
The goddam phone rang.
I said that miserable no good Alexander Graham Bell.
I said that meddling old bastard.
Betsy giggled.
Then she sat down and doubled up laughing.
Sometimes whores are hard to figure out.
They got that much in common with call girls.

Betsy blew in at three twenty-two.

I just happened to notice.

I pretended I was asleep.

Betsy slipped into bed.

She was very warm and very soft and very smooth.

She started biting on my shoulder and blowing on my neck.

It was probably the blowing on my neck that did it.

About four o'clock Betsy said Chance you're just a big pushover.

I shrugged.

I said I ought to be.

I said I work very hard at it.

Betsy said tell me something.

She said are you getting over Candi Yakozi?

I shrugged.

I said Candi who?

Betsy said I see that you don't even know her.

100

I said that's right.

Betsy said believe me you really don't.

She said Candi does weird things.

I said like go to bed with private detectives.

Betsy said oh worse than that.

Betsy said once she took the garbage out while wearing nothing but her panties.

She said at noon.

I said well it beats going out stark naked.

Betsy said not by much.

Betsy said you know what kind of panties Candi wears.

I shrugged.

I said as a matter of fact I didn't even know she wore panties.

Betsy winced.

She said I guess I asked for that.

I said it's a wonder she didn't get raped or arrested.

Betsy said she did.

I said which?

Betsy said she got raped by the cops who arrested her.

I said speaking of rape there is some old woman who is raping bartenders.

Betsy said that's utterly impossible.

I shrugged.

I said okay.

I said let's get some sleep.

Betsy said why don't we have a good-night cigarette first?

We had a whole bunch of good-night cigarettes.

Dawn was breaking when Winston chirped us to sleep from the window ledge.

Betsy is sort of wonderful to be with.

Betsy went out on a call that Saturday.

I bought a carton of Camels at Mama Rosa's grocery store.

Mama Rosa didn't know anybody named Nivlek Ysteb.

I got a haircut at Kelvin and Armitage.

The barber didn't know anybody named Nivlek Ysteb.

I got five dollars' worth of gas.

The station attendant didn't know anybody named Nivlek Ysteb.

There wasn't much doing at Wallace's.

Old Dad Underwood was sitting at the bar.

He was trying to stand a dime on edge.

Wallace watched him suspiciously.

Old Dad Underwood said oncet I knowed a feller what could stand a razor blade on edge.

102

Wallace said before or after he shaved with it?
Old Dad Underwood said I never asked him.
Wallace said well you should of.
He said that's important.
I ordered a schooner of beer.
Wallace said my head aches so bad my goddam belt
uckle hurts.
I said you ever hear of somebody named Nivlek Ysteb?
Wallace scratched his head.
He shrunk from the pain.
He said not that I know of.
He said last year I met three guys named Zunk.
I said it is probably very unusual to meet even one guy
amed Zunk.
Wallace said these was brothers.
He said they got a truck farm out on Bloomingdale
oad.
He said they call it Zunk's Bloomingdale Road Truck
arm.
Old Dad Underwood slipped his dime into his pocket.
He came over and sat beside me.
I bought him a beer.
He said names is funny things.
Wallace nodded.
He gritted his teeth in agony.
Old Dad Underwood said now you take the name of
mith.
He said I ain't never knowed nobody named Smith.
He said I still don't know nobody named Smith.
I said not knowing somebody named Smith is also
robably very unusual.
I said why it may be even more unusual than meeting
ree guys named Zunk.
Old Dad Underwood said by Christ you are beyond
oubt one hunnert goddam absolutely percent correct.
Wallace said oh I wouldn't go quite that far.
He said just look in the phone book.
He said for every goddam Smith which is in there I

will show you forty-five goddam Zunks which ain't there.

Old Dad Underwood said how you going to show me forty-five goddam Zunks which ain't in there if they ain't even in there in the firstest place?

Wallace said I think perhaps you better get back to whatever it was you wasn't making no goddam sense in the second place.

Old Dad Underwood said all right I am undoubtedly the only man in the country what don't know nobody named Smith.

He said I used to lay awake of nights just praying I would meet somebody named Smith.

He said this was all on account of I wanted to be like other people.

Old Dad Underwood shot a defiant forefinger into the air.

His voice swelled to a shout of triumph.

He said them days is gone forever.

He said my friends I am here to tell you that things has changed.

He said now I don't never want to meet nobody named Smith.

He said all them goddam Smiths can just get in line to kiss my ass.

Old Dad Underwood smote the bar with the flat of his hand.

It made a sharp spanging sound.

Like a ninety-millimeter gun.

Wallace recoiled.

He glared at Old Dad Underwood.

He said you do that just one more time and I am going to throw your goddam ass out in the middle of the goddam street.

Old Dad Underwood ignored Wallace.

He said now I can dare to be different.

He said just wait till you are seventy.

He said you too will dare to be different.

Wallace said why do we just not change the goddam subject?

He said maybe we ought to talk about ESP or something.

Old Dad Underwood said that ESP just ain't no good.

He said I knowed a feller what put a can in his car and now his radio don't work no more.

Wallace looked at me with beseeching eyes.

He said there just ain't no way I deserve this.

Old Dad Underwood said he poured it right in the radiator too.

Wallace said I ain't never hurt nobody in my whole goddam life.

He picked up my glass and shuffled sadly away to the tap.

I said forget it Wallace.

I said I got to get back to the temple of love.

Old Dad Underwood said I heard all about them there kinds of places.

He said I knowed a feller what went in one called the Passion Spa.

He said they had to take him out on a stretcher.

Wallace's saddle-brown eyes lit up.

He said hot damn what happened?

Old Dad Underwood said he fell down the stairs and busted his leg.

Wallace leaned on the beer spout.

He said I am going to sell this joint and get drunk forever.

Old Dad Underwood said if I was you I would try something I never done before.

I left.

On the way home I pulled up at Mama Rosa's grocery store.

Mama Rosa still didn't know anybody named Nivlek Ysteb.

I bought a package of bubble gum.

That way the day wasn't completely wasted.

> *... firstest wives never lasts as long as sec-*
> *ondest wives ... until they becomes sec-*
> *ondest wives. ...*

Betsy fixed pork chops and scalloped potatoes that evening.

After coffee I gave her a hand with the dishes.

Betsy said what should we do tonight?

I said how about a movie?

Betsy said I thought we might stay home and enjoy some stimulating conversation.

I said it just so happens that I was involved in some stimulating conversation a little earlier in the day.

I said it stimulated me to come home.

I said you want some bubble gum?

Betsy said I mean stimulating conversation about us getting married.

I said somehow I do not find this sort of conversation to be particularly stimulating.

Betsy folded the dish towel.

She draped it over the sink.

She gave me a nice level look.

She said we will be married someday.

I said the meek will inherit the earth someday.

I went into the living room.

I sat on the couch.

Betsy brought me a beer.

She sat beside me.

She put her arm around me.

She said Chance I believe you're afraid to get married.

I said I got a right to be afraid.

I said I got a right to be rigid with terror.

Betsy said you never told me what happened during your first marriage.

I said I don't like the way you emphasized first marriage.

I said you seemed to imply that there could be a second.

Betsy said so tell me.

I said maybe I better tell you what didn't happen.

I said that way we might get to bed by midnight.

Betsy said did she drink a lot?

I said was Hitler a Nazi a lot?

Betsy said did she sleep around?

I said well let's just say she had a split personality.

I said one-half nympho and one-half maniac.

Betsy said where is she now?

I said I don't know and nobody better never ever tell me.

Betsy went to the closet and took out a jacket.

She said what movie do you have in mind?

I shrugged.

*...lastest western movie I seen they let
me in for free ... cost me fourteen dollars
to get out....*

MONROE D. UNDERWOOD

We ended up at a western.
Showdown in Sundown City.
Or some goddam thing.
I fell asleep during the big shoot-out.
On the way home Betsy said the good guys won it.
I said that figures.
I said they got a big edge in the series.
I said God is always on their side that's why.

Monday morning Betsy had a call in Arlington Heights.
When she left I had three cups of coffee and a brain-
storm.
I looked in the telephone book for Ystebs.
I found one.
3442 West Belmont Avenue.
I dialed the number.
A woman answered.
I said is Nivlek there?
The woman said who this?
I had to think fast.
I said Boris.
She said Boris who?
I said Stranguloff.
She said I don't know nobody named Stranguloff.
She said I don't even know nobody named Boris.
I said what about Nivlek?
She said I don't know nobody named Nivlek.

I said do you know anybody named Smith?
She said no.
I said neither does Old Dad Underwood.
She said I don't know nobody named Underwood.

. . . oncet I knowed a feller what could imitate a butterfly on the telephone . . . fooled me every goddam time . . . never did explain how he done it. . . .

MONROE D. UNDERWOOD

An hour or so later the phone rang.
I picked it up.
A deep voice said Betsy?
I said oh yes.
I said is that you Henrietta?
The line went dead.

*. . . only Smiths I ever heard of was John
and Al . . . some injun woman saved John
. . . wasn't nobody could of helped Al. . . .*

MONROE D. UNDERWOOD

I found a suburban telephone book in a drugstore.
No Ystebs.
I called the plumbers' union.
No Ystebs.
I called the Brotherhood of Railroad Trainmen.
A grouchy bastard said we don't got no Ystebs.
He told me they had almost two hundred Smiths.

> *...oncet I knowed a feller what under-*
> *stood women ... never did get married for*
> *some reason....*
>
> MONROE D. UNDERWOOD

That night Betsy and I went to one of those old-fashioned pubs for a hamburger and a beer.
Betsy had the hamburger.
I had the beer.
I said do you know anybody named Nivlek Ysteb?
Betsy said should I?
I said how the hell would I know?
Betsy gave me a funny look.
She said by God I think I'll have a beer.

> ... *just don't pay to be too skeptical* ...
> *oncet I knowed a feller what claimed to*
> *be Jesus Christ* ... *he took a quart of wine*
> *to the men's room* ... *came back with a*
> *quart of water* ... *that kind of carrying on*
> *makes a feller stop and think.* ...
>
> MONROE D. UNDERWOOD

On Friday morning I drove to Elmwood Park.

There was nothing but my pay in the post office box.

I stuck the envelope in my pocket and headed for Wallace's.

Wallace was slumped against the backbar.

He was shaking his head from side to side.

Like a bull when it sees a red flag.

He said I am going to peddle this joint and move to Alaska.

He said I am going to open a whole bunch of gold mines.

I said you already got a gold mine.

Wallace said yes but this particular gold mine is in Chicago.

114

He said I get these here awful headaches in Chicago you see.

I said just a minute Wallace.

I said could there be the slightest possibility that strong drink might be related to your problem?

Wallace said drinking ain't got absolutely nothing to do with it.

He said it is the air pollution and them Sox.

Shorty Connors came in.

Shorty Connors stood about six feet six.

He was called Shorty because his brother stood about six feet nine.

Shorty Connors was carrying a battered old cornet.

Wallace approached Shorty Connors very cautiously.

The way you approach a wounded rhinoceros.

He lowered his voice to a confidential level.

He said Shorty just what do you figure on doing with that goddam old cornet?

Shorty Connors smiled mysteriously.

He said now that ain't a very smart question.

He said what do people usually do with goddam old cornets?

Wallace said well in Wallace's tavern they usually get them shoved up their rear ends.

He said particularly if they blow them.

Shorty Connors said please stand back.

He said I am about to rip off a few rousing choruses of "Tie Me to Your Goddam Apron Strings Again."

He said plus "The Goddam Rose of Tralee."

He said also "The Flight of the Goddam Bumblebee."

Wallace nodded.

He put his hands on his hips.

He said leave us not rush blindly forward all barriers disregarding.

He said I am about to make you the best offer you ever got in your whole life.

He said if you will not cut loose on that goddam fish

horn I will not put you in some intensive-care ward for about seventeen years.

Wallace bought a round to prove his good intentions.

Shorty Connors winked at me.

He said I ain't bought a drink since back last October.

He said all I need is this here good old cornet.

I said you play that thing?

Shorty Connors frowned.

He said I kind of doubt it.

He said I ain't never tried.

Old Dad Underwood came in.

He looked at the cornet.

He said oncet I knowed a feller what had two of them there contraptions spliced to one mouthpiece.

He said this here feller played "Roses of Picardy" with one hand and "When My Baby Smiles at Me" with the other.

Wallace uttered a naughty word.

Old Dad Underwood said oh my God it was just plumb beautiful.

He said it touched these here old heartstrings.

He said it brung tears to these old eyes.

Wallace snorted.

He said you ain't never seen no such goddam goddam thing.

He said ain't nobody ever had that much wind.

He said except probably you.

He said you got enough wind to inflate a couple dozen dirigibles.

Old Dad Underwood said speaking of dirigibles I seen the *Akron* and the *Macon* and the *Los Angeles* and the *Shenandoah* and the *Von Hitlerburg*.

He said they was all out at the Mahoning County Fair back in Ohio oncet.

He said they was doing these here stunts.

He said loop-the-loops and barrel rolls and tailspins and them there things.

He said they was just carrying on something fierce.

He said I was ever so impressed.

Wallace looked at me.

He said my goddam reward got to be in heaven.

He said me and Job and all them guys.

Shorty Connors beat me out of a cigarette.

He said by the way I hear tell you are looking for a man named Vostek or something.

I said yeah.

Shorty Connors said a few weeks back we took in a roomer with a name like that.

I felt the hair on the back of my neck begin to stand up.

Shorty Connors said Melvin Yostev.

I said could it be Nivlek Ysteb?

Shorty Connors said well yes.

He said it could also be Hernando Morales.

He said but it's Melvin Yostev.

I felt the hair on the back of my neck begin to go limp.

Shorty Connors said of course I ain't about to take no oaths on nothing.

He said I can't hardly even read this guy's handwriting.

He said why I remember when the army had me down as O'Connell.

He said I had to reenlist six times to get it changed.

He said we worked out a compromise.

He said they made it Connerly.

He said come to think of it Melvin Yostev sounds a whole lot like Nivlek Ysteb.

He said not exactly but goddam near almost.

I said what sort of character is this roomer?

Shorty Connors said he is a strange little bastard but he don't bother nobody.

He said he claims to be a painter but he don't never paint nothing.

He said he just stays in his room all day.

He said only time he ever goes out is around midnight.

He said he don't hardly ever get back until like three in the morning.

I could feel the hair on the back of my neck begin to stand up.

I said do you know where he comes from?

Shorty Connors said he told me Cleveland but he talks better English than that.

> ... *oncet I knowed a feller what had seven*
> *sons . . . named all of them Horatio . . .*
> *soon as they growed up they lynched*
> *him. . . .*
>
> MONROE D. UNDERWOOD

Shorty Connors lived at 3008 Palmer Avenue.
I found that out by looking for Deuteronomy Connors
in the telephone book.
That's Shorty's first name.
Deuteronomy.
Shorty hardly ever uses it.

> *... chess is a game what is kind of like checkers only you play it sort of different. ...*
>
> MONROE D. UNDERWOOD

❋

I parked a few doors east of 3008 Palmer Avenue at ten forty-five that night.

I smoked cigarettes and listened to *Alte Kameraden* on my tape player.

I watched the front door like a hawk.

A scrawny guy came out a few minutes before midnight.

He headed east.

When he had gone a half-block I got out and followed.

He walked over to California Avenue.

He went into a little tavern under the elevated line.

He nodded to the bartender.

He bought a schooner of beer.

He sat at a table in a corner.

I took a seat at the bar.

I ordered a double Jack Daniels.

I studied the scrawny guy.

He looked like a cross between a chicken-killing weasel and a weasel-killing chicken.

He kept glancing toward the door like he was expecting somebody.

He was.

In a few minutes a big shaggy-haired guy came in.

He wore thick mad-scientist glasses and he carried an attaché case.

He sat at the table with the scrawny guy.

He took a pint of Comrade Terrorist vodka from his coat pocket.

He drank half of it in one gulp.

He opened the attaché case and took out a chess set.

By closing time they had played seven games.

The scrawny guy destroyed the big shaggy-haired guy seven times.

He launched his attack from a king's knight's gambit.

He was a slashing and merciless surgeon at the chessboard.

When they were finished the scrawny guy took a small piece of paper from his wallet.

He handed it to the big shaggy-haired guy.

He said maybe this one bit too difficult for you.

The big shaggy-haired guy glanced at it.

He laughed a cruel raspy laugh.

He slipped the paper into his pocket.

He took his chess set and went out.

I finished my severalth double Jack Daniels and followed the scrawny guy.

He walked directly back to 3008 Palmer Avenue.

He walked a lot more directly back to 3008 Palmer Avenue than I did.

I couldn't find my car.

I finally found the damn thing.

It was right where I had left it.

It wouldn't start.

I cussed it out.

It still wouldn't start.

The battery was dead.
I went looking for a phone.
I found a telephone booth up on Fullerton Avenue.
I called Betsy.
Betsy said where the hell are you?
I said I am in a telephone booth.
Betsy said I understand that.
She said but where the hell is the telephone booth?
I said on Fullerton Avenue.
Betsy said Chance Fullerton Avenue is ten miles long.
I said I am across the street from a Shell gas station.
Betsy said what does it say on the Shell gas station sign?
I said it says Shell.
Betsy said oh Jesus.
I said there is another sign.
Betsy said well thank the good Lord.
She said what does it say?
I said it says tuneups.
I said it also says brakes.
Betsy swore.
She said how did you get there?
I said I walked.
Betsy said where the hell is your automobile?
I said at 3008 Palmer Avenue.
I said it won't start.
I said the battery is dead.
I said I left the goddam lights on.
I said come and get me.
Betsy said you are smashed.
I said well sweetheart it all comes under the heading of another night's work for the gool ole Unitensnates of America Gol Bess her.
I sang "Gol Bess America."
Betsy said keep singing and I'll find you.
I was still singing when Betsy got there.
Betsy rolled a window down.
She said hang up the phone and come out of that booth.

I couldn't find the door.

Betsy got out and opened it for me.

I said that goddam thing is a death trap.

I said a man could starve to death in there.

Betsy said I have cables in the trunk.

She said do you want a jump?

I said you are certainly a very pragmasticated broad.

Betsy said I am talking about getting your car started you drunken ass.

I said why do we not just proclasnitate until tomorrow?

I said nobody is going to steal it.

I said it won't start.

I said the battery is dead.

Betsy said I'll bet you left the lights on.

On the way home I sang "You're a Gran Ole Frag."

I have an excellent voice for patriotic numbers.

I told Betsy this.

I didn't mince words.

I said Betsy I have an excellnet voice for paritomic munders.

Betsy didn't say anything.

. . . oncet I knowed a feller what woke up without a hangover . . . called an ambulance . . . thought he was dying. . . .

MONROE D. UNDERWOOD

Betsy got me up about ten.

On the kitchen table she had a hot buttered cinnamon roll and ice-cold orange juice and scalding black coffee and the Chicago *Sun-Times.*

During my third cup of coffee Betsy said Chance I hope you aren't doing anything dangerous.

I shrugged.

I said my God so the hell do I.

I was staring at the Chicago *Sun-Times* headline.

An FBI agent had been found stabbed to death in Grant Park.

I remembered the big shaggy-haired guy's cruel raspy laugh.

*...why sure there is conservative writers
...who the hell you think wrote them
there Dead Sea Scrolls?...*

MONROE D. UNDERWOOD

I trailed the scrawny guy again that night.
Same time.
Same route.
Same tavern.
Same big shaggy-haired guy.
More chess.
Another piece of paper.
Another cruel raspy laugh.
The next morning the Chicago *Sun-Times* reported that a conservative writer had been run over by a moving van.
This came as a very great shock to me.
I hadn't known that there were any conservative writers.

*... to err is human ... oncet I had a parrot
what kept saying that. ...*

MONROE D. UNDERWOOD

The next night the scrawny guy didn't go into the little tavern under the elevated line.

He ducked into an alley a few doors south of the tavern.

It was a very dark alley.

I hummed a bit of *Alte Kameraden*.

I followed him in.

He vanished around a corner of a building.

When I made the turn he was waiting for me.

He was pointing an accusing finger in my direction.

He said this is man who all the time following me every night.

Two shadowy figures came at me out of the darkness.

I didn't hesitate.

I hit the first shadowy figure right between the eyes.

I stepped over him.

I hit the second shadowy figure right between the eyes.

I stepped over him.

I looked for the scrawny guy.
I wanted to hit him right between the eyes.
The scrawny guy wasn't there.
He was out on California Avenue.
He was hollering help police and any number of ridiculous things.

> ... it is nice to get together with the old
> gang now and then . . . even if the old
> gang don't appreciate it....
>
> MONROE D. UNDERWOOD

❦

At the Shakespeare police station Kellis J. Ammson did
not look a great deal like Kellis J. Ammson.

He bore a closer resemblance to a raccoon.

This was because he had two black eyes.

Kellis J. Ammson was on his knees before the grizzled
old desk sergeant.

His arms were outstretched.

His eyes were rolled heavenward.

The grizzled old desk sergeant looked up from his
crossword puzzle.

He said you sing just one note of "Mammy" and I will
lock your ass up.

Kellis J. Ammson said is there no flaming balm in
Gilead?

The grizzled old desk sergeant said I am unable to say
but there is a Super-Kola machine in the hall.

He said you got to have exact change.

128

Kellis J. Ammson said oh surely flaming justice will triumph tonight.

The grizzled old desk sergeant said well that will be simply super because the Cubs lost this afternoon.

He said the Sox got rained out.

He said they always get rained out in Oakland.

I said I thought I was going to be liquidated.

Gino Scarletti was sitting on a bench.

His walrus moustache was tousled.

He had two black eyes.

He said mother marrone.

The scrawny guy said I am got to hire private detectives because this is man who all the time following me every night.

I said what was on those little pieces of paper?

The scrawny guy said chess problems dumbbell.

I said up your king's knight's gambit.

The grizzled old desk sergeant sighed.

He stood up.

He pointed to the door.

Very majestically.

Like Caesar at the Forum or someplace.

He said that will be all.

He said out.

He said everybody out.

He said I got a whole lot better ways to spend my time.

He said I got seniority.

He said I got connections.

He said I got a brother-in-law shook hands with Mayor Daley.

He said I don't got to put up with this kind of crap.

He said out goddammit.

We filed out.

The scrawny guy walked behind me.

He tugged at my sleeve.

He said hey you playing chess?

I shrugged.

I said well not exactly.

The scrawny guy said okay but I buying you beer any-way.

We walked up to the little tavern under the elevated line.

We had a few beers.

He wasn't a bad sort.

He was a painter.

His name was Melvin Yostev.

He was from Cleveland.

> ...the best laid plans of mice and men
> gang aft agley ... feller what said that got
> a cigar named after him ... might of done
> even better if he could of spoke En-
> glish....
>
> *MONROE D. UNDERWOOD*

✾

Betsy was going down to Mama Rosa's grocery store
the next morning.

She said why don't you come along?

I said before I would go shopping with a woman I
would climb Mount Everest.

I said in the nude.

I said in January.

I said blindfolded.

I said at midnight.

I said carrying a grand piano.

I said besides I got other plans.

When Betsy left I called Candi Yakozi.

I said do you know anybody named Ysteb?

Candi said is it terribly important?

I said damn right.

Candi said would you believe that I know just oodles
of Ystebs?

She said come right over.
I said are any of them named Nivlek?
Candi said is that important too?
I said very.
Candi said oh my goodness gracious what an astounding coincidence.
She said as a matter of fact almost all of them are named Nivlek.
She said hurry over and you'll get steak and eggs.
She said steak and eggs isn't all you're going to get.
I took a shower and dressed.
I met Betsy at the bottom of the stairs.
She was carrying a bulging shopping bag.
She said where are you going?
I said I am going out for steak and eggs.
Betsy said go back upstairs.
She said I just bought steak and eggs.
She said steak and eggs isn't all you're going to get.

> ... oncet I knowed a feller what smuggled
> a ham into a synagogue ... only man what
> ever got circumised twenty-two times. ...
>
> MONROE D. UNDERWOOD

I had three cups of black coffee while Betsy fried the steak.

Betsy said did you hear the telephone this morning?

I said no who was it?

Betsy winked at me.

She said Kellis J. Ammson.

I said how did he get this number?

Betsy winked at me.

She said he's a detective.

She said Ammson wants to hire you back.

She said at five hundred dollars per week.

She said he seems to think it might be better for all concerned.

She said he told me he has a very hot international case for you.

I said I don't need a very hot international case.

I said I already got a very hot international case.

Betsy said he told me this has to do with smuggling.
I said smuggling what?
Betsy winked at me.
She said I think he said mushrooms.
She said into the Black Forest.
I said tell Ammson I am otherwise occupied.
I said tell him I am on a big United States government thing.
I said I got to find Nivlek Ysteb that sonofabitch.
Betsy winked at me.
She said don't make snap judgments.
She said Nivlek Ysteb just might be a very nice person.
She smiled an impish smile.
She winked at me again.
I said Betsy you better get that eye examined.
The steak and eggs hit the spot.
Steak and eggs wasn't all I got.

. . . there is better things to do than just sit
around drinking . . . name one. . . .

MONROE D. UNDERWOOD

Betsy had a call that afternoon.
I said I think I'll go over to Wallace's and have a few.
Betsy said why don't I just drop you off at Wallace's?
She said I'll pick you up coming back.
She said that way both of us can have a few.
I shrugged.

... oncet I knowed a feller what wrote a song about the Gobi Desert ... don't recall him making much money on it....

MONROE D. UNDERWOOD

❈

Wallace was a little under the weather.

He popped for a bottle of beer.

He said I feel terrible.

He said I am going to dump this den of unspeakable iniquity.

He said I am going to move to Wyoming and raise mountain lions.

I said is there a booming market for mountain lions?

Wallace said I don't know about that but they don't got no air pollution in Wyoming.

He said it's the air pollution gives me these here headaches.

He said air pollution and them Sox.

I nodded.

I said I understand all about that part.

I said the part I don't understand all about is the part about the mountain lions.

Wallace said well I got to do something with my time.

He said why I could go bananas just sitting around on some goddam mountaintop.

He said a man should consider things like that.

I said you know it never entered my mind.

It started to rain.

There was big thunder to the west.

Old Dad Underwood came stomping in.

He kicked a barstool.

He said &@#$%¢*!

Wallace said don't kick that barstool and stop saying &@#$%¢*!

Old Dad Underwood said don't mess with me sonny.

He said I am in one highly dangerous state of mind.

He said I may just kill somebody.

Wallace said what's the matter did somebody steal your mineral oil?

Old Dad Underwood said I will tell you what's the matter.

He said I just met some dirty sonofabitch named Smith that's what's the matter.

He said now my record is busted all to smithereens.

He said now I ain't nothing but just another goddam has-been.

Wallace said ah it was ever thus.

He said fame is but a fleeting thing.

Old Dad Underwood said you can just knock off all that philosophy jazz and get me a beer.

Wallace said well cheer up.

He said you still ain't met nobody named Ignatz Riffniak.

Old Dad Underwood said that's on account of there ain't nobody named Ignatz Riffniak.

He said you just made that name up.

Wallace said yes and that ain't all.

He said I also just made up a song.

He said this song is about Wyoming.

Old Dad Underwood said somebody already made up a song about Wyoming.

Wallace said well that don't bother me none nohow.

He said look at all them songs somebody made up about Ohio.

He said the name of my song is "When the Golden Beer is Foaming in Wyoming."

Old Dad Underwood said oh Jesus Christ.

Wallace fixed Old Dad Underwood with a gimlet eye.

He said all right wise guy let's just see you make up a song.

Old Dad Underwood said I heard somewheres Wyoming is a dry state.

He said hell a man can get a drink in Ohio.

Betsy came in.

She sat in a booth.

I bought her a highball and sat with her.

I said I thought you had a call.

Betsy said I got rained out.

I said how can a whore get rained out?

Betsy's eyes flashed.

I said how can a call girl get rained out?

Betsy said he wanted to go in the grape arbor.

I said that don't make no sense.

I said the grapes aren't even ripe yet.

I said what was wrong with the bedroom?

Betsy said his wife was painting it.

I said maybe we better go before something terrible happens.

Betsy said why don't we wait until I finish my highball?

I said by that time it may be too goddam late.

Betsy finished her highball.

It was too goddam late.

Wallace sang "When the Golden Beer is Foaming in Wyoming":

> When the golden beer is foaming in Wyoming
> That's when I'll be coming home to you
> Little sweetheart of the great big canyon
> We will have a brew or maybe even two.

138

I said my God Betsy why don't you ever listen to me?

Betsy applauded Wallace's performance.

Wallace turned beet-red with pleasure.

He sang "When the Golden Beer is Foaming in Wyoming" again.

During the encore Old Dad Underwood fled the premises.

Beer streamed from his moustache.

Betsy said oh Wallace that was simply beautiful.

She said so sentimental.

She blew Wallace a kiss.

Wallace broke a quart of Jack Daniels.

*... oncet I rode with a woman driver ... I
gonna tell you flat out oncet was aplenty
... we was in a funeral procession yet. ...*

MONROE D. UNDERWOOD

We drove homeward through heavy gray rain.
The traffic moved sluggishly.
Betsy didn't.
Betsy drives like an utter maniac.
No offense to utter maniacs intended.
Some of my best friends are utter maniacs.
Betsy glanced at me.
She said a penny for your thoughts.
I shrugged.
I said I was just thinking.
I said I was just thinking of the great rapport existent
between you and this overpowered vehicle.
I said it is uncanny.
I said I am awestricken.
I said I am so goddam awestricken that I will thank
you to let me off at the next corner.
I said I will flag down a meteor or a comparable means
of safe conveyance.

140

Betsy said stop crossing yourself.
She said you aren't even Catholic.
She said besides we're almost home.
I said the Germans were almost to Moscow.
Betsy slowed down.
The last twenty blocks took nearly a minute.

When Betsy came out of the bedroom I was sitting on
the couch.

I was reading a copy of *Eagles* magazine.

Betsy was wearing powder-blue pajamas.

Very sheer.

Betsy picked up the newspaper and curled herself into
a big chair.

Like all the beautiful cats in the world.

After a few minutes she said I see here that necro-
philes can now go to heaven.

I said who says so?

Betsy said the National Unified Council of Churches.

I said does God know about this?

Betsy said it doesn't say.

She said what is that you're reading?

I said something of consequence.

I said *Eagles* magazine.

Betsy said oh that's just an old pulp thing.

She said my grandfather always read that stuff.

She said where do you get them?

I said this place in New York got about a million of them.

I said get a load of this.

I read to Betsy from "Hell in the Clouds" by Arch Blockhouse:

Biff Brimstone kicked left rudder savagely. He jammed the stick against the instrument panel. The golden Spad heeled over and slammed out of the sun down down down in the wake of the frantically fleeing fuchsia Fokker. The wind wailed through the brace wires like berserk banshees. Biff Brimstone hit the triggers and the Vickers twin machine guns yammered out their doubly deadly diabolical duet of death.

I grinned at Betsy.

I said how about that kiddo?

Betsy yawned.

She said Chance what do berserk banshees sound like?

I shrugged.

I said probably something like wind wailing through brace wires.

Betsy snapped her fingers like a craps shooter.

She said why of course.

She said I should have known that.

She went back to her newspaper.

The thunder rumbled and crackled.

Lightning hung in the dark sky like bright broken worms.

Betsy leaned back and stretched.

When Betsy leans back and stretches any number of interesting things happen.

Betsy folded her newspaper.

She dropped it on the floor beside her chair.

She said it will probably rain forever.

143

She said let's get drunk.

I closed the *Eagles* magazine.

I looked Betsy right in the eye.

I said Betsy getting drunk is retreating from reality.

I said it is candid acknowledgement that we are no longer capable of coping with our problems.

I said it is surrender pure and simple.

Betsy said look do you want to get drunk or don't you?

I said you better believe it.

Betsy went into the kitchen.

She was back in a trice with an ice bucket and a quart of vodka.

I said Betsy how long is a trice?

Betsy said I have no idea.

She said why?

I said you were back in a trice.

Betsy placed the ice and the bottle of vodka on the coffee table.

She said what else do we need?

I said I could sure use a glass.

Betsy said I'll be back in half-a-trice.

> ...when I stop to think of all them there
> things I allus wanted to do it brings to
> mind all them there things I never got
> done....
>
> MONROE D. UNDERWOOD

❀

'An hour later the thunder and lightning were gone.
There was only the steady flailing rain.
The FM purred "Moonlight Serenade."
Then "Deep Purple."
Then "Falling Leaves."
Betsy said oh isn't this cozy?
She said with the storm out there and you in here.
She said right where you belong.
She said with me.
I said I got to admit I've made worse stops.
Betsy said tell me about this Nivlek Ysteb.
I shrugged.

145

I said I just got to find him that's all.

I said the United States government wants him.

I said Nivlek Ysteb is a bad mother.

Betsy said what happens when you finish the job?

I said the government gets Ysteb.

Betsy said then what?

I shrugged.

I said I don't like to think about then what.

I said Ysteb is all that stands between me and punching a clock in some goddam factory.

I said remind me to thank him for the reprieve.

Betsy said Chance if you weren't a detective what would you like to be?

I shrugged.

I said smart I guess.

Betsy said oh come on now.

I said I don't want to tell you.

I said you'll think I'm nuts.

Betsy said no I won't.

She said we've all had our pipe dreams.

She said would you believe that I always wanted to join the Salvation Army?

She laughed a short hard laugh.

She said oh dear God.

I said well you'd sure have to change uniforms.

Betsy said now tell me about you.

I said I think I'd like to own a little neighborhood tavern.

Betsy winked at me.

She said something like Wallace's I'll bet.

I shrugged.

I said yeah sort of.

I said if I owned one the very first thing I'd do would be put *Alte Kameraden* on the jukebox.

Betsy winked at me.

She said when you get your tavern can I help you with it?

She said I'd make one hell of a barmaid.
I said well don't buy any aprons just yet.
Betsy winked at me again.
I could see that her eye wasn't improving much.

Late that afternoon the rain packed up and moved east.
The sun came out just in time to go down.
The vodka bottle was empty.
I walked over to the window.
I nodded to Winston on the window ledge.
I stood there looking out.
Betsy said what are you doing?
I said I am looking out of the window.
Betsy said well you certainly fooled me.
She said I would have sworn you were playing poker with an iguana.
I said iguanas are lousy poker players.
I said they aren't much at dominoes either.
Betsy said what I meant was what are you looking at?
I said a black '74 Mercury parked just north of my car.
I said there are two guys in it.
Betsy said what are they doing?
I shrugged.

I said well from here it would appear that they are sitting in a black '74 Mercury parked just north of my car.

Betsy said will you please stop being silly?

I said it's a tough habit to kick.

Betsy winked at me.

She said perhaps Nivlek Ysteb is in the car.

She giggled.

I said look that's not funny.

I said that Communist bastard might blow up your apartment.

I said you just put up these new drapes and everything.

Betsy winked at me.

Betsy said Chance I believe you'll find Nivlek Ysteb where you least expect.

I shrugged.

I said when I get him do you know what I'm going to do?

I took a deep breath.

Like before a dose of castor oil.

I blurted it out.

I said I'm going to marry you.

Betsy jumped up.

She said I am going out for more vodka.

She said get me U-Haul's number quick.

I said I'm not drunk.

I said I'm tired of running in circles.

Betsy said well so am I.

I said I never knew a man who married a whore.

Betsy didn't correct me.

She laughed instead.

She said Chance you've never known a man who didn't marry a whore.

She said all women are whores.

She said every woman has her price.

She said money or thrills or status or revenge or whatever.

She said we're for sale sweetheart.

She came over to the window.

She put an arm around me.

Winston hopped around nervously.

He chirped a few bars of *Alte Kameraden*.

He hit a clinker or two but he gave it a pretty good shot.

Betsy looked up at me.

She said Chance would you really marry me?

I shrugged.

I said why the hell not?

I said a factory worker needs a lunch-packer.

Betsy winked at me.

She said maybe it won't come to a factory job.

She said perhaps there is a better way.

She winked at me again.

I said I'm worried about that eye of yours.

Betsy kissed me.

She said last one in bed is a sissy.

Living with Betsy wasn't all that bad.

Betsy and I spent the next day just loafing around the
apartment.

Winston sat on the window ledge and preened.

Betsy didn't get any calls.

That night we played casino.

Betsy is a terrific casino player.

I ate a slice of chocolate fudge cake.

I had a few cans of beer.

I listened to *Alte Kameraden* on Betsy's big set.

Betsy said where does Winston go at night?

I shrugged.

I said I never meddle in his affairs.

I read a story in *Eagles* magazine.

About nine o'clock I called D. L. Ambercrombie.

He said did you find any of that marked money yet?

I said no but I'm working on it.

Ambercrombie said Purdue you are a damn good man.

When I hung up I was smiling.

I called Booligan.

Booligan said did you locate that crazy old broad yet?

I said no but I'm working on it.

Booligan said Purdue you are an utterly worthless sonofabitch.

When I hung up I was frowning.

Betsy was watching me.

She said woe unto you when all men shall speak well of you.

I said where did you get that?

Betsy said from Luke.

I said if he's a customer you better be careful.

I said he talks funny.

Betsy said Luke in the Bible.

I said maybe you ought to start thinking seriously about the Salvation Army.

I said you'd make field marshal overnight.

I said when you are field marshal you could have the band play *Alte Kameraden*.

Betsy got a call about eleven o'clock.

I said what time will you be back?

Betsy said oh one o'clock or so.

I said I think I'll go over to Wallace's for a nightcap.

... one thing what you can bet on ... you can bet there ain't no woman what you can bet on....

❖

When I entered Wallace's I found Wallace sitting on the floor behind the bar.

He looked dazed.

He was missing some hair.

His face was scratched.

His lower lip was swollen.

He said I just been raped.

I said Wallace don't let this destroy you.

I said you will rise above this.

I said it is always darkest before the dawn.

I said time heals everything.

Wallace said hold the onward and upward baloney.

He said catch that old woman.

He said she went out the back door.

He said I am going to sell this joint.

He said I am going to Turkey where I will raise about ten million acres of goddam opium poppies.

I went through the back door on the double.

153

An old woman was leaving the alley.
I caught up with her.
I grabbed her arm.
She turned.
She smiled sweetly.
She said why Mr. Purdue.
She belted me alongside the head with her purse.
She must have had an anvil in it.

*. . . I never knowed a solution what ever
solved anything yet. . . .*

MONROE D. UNDERWOOD

❈

When all the colored lights stopped flashing I sat up.
A piece of paper was sticking out of my shoe.
I unfolded it.
It was a fifty-dollar bill.
Ulysses S. Grant had a red moustache.
I staggered back to Wallace's.
Wallace was on his feet.
He said well it wasn't a total loss.
He said she left me five dollars.
I said give me some change for the telephone.
I rubbed my scalp where the hair was missing.
The scratches on my face burned.
I licked my swollen lower lip.
I called D. L. Ambercrombie and Booligan.
I told them about Myrtle Culpepper.

*... sure wisht I had all that there drinking
time I wasted just sleeping. ...*

MONROE D. UNDERWOOD

Betsy held the ice bag to my head.
She said try to forget it Chance.
I said she seemed like such a nice old broad.
Betsy said all you need is sleep.
I said how can I sleep after this?
Betsy said let me show you.
She said come to bed.
She said baby I'll put you to sleep.
Betsy put me to sleep in a hurry.

...you give some women six inches and they want a mile....

MONROE D. UNDERWOOD

�462

Betsy woke me up late the following morning.

She handed me a lighted Camel and a cup of black coffee and the Chicago *Sun-Times*.

She said take a look at the front page.

I did.

I saw a picture of Myrtle Culpepper.

The accompanying article said that Myrtle Culpepper was probably a crusader.

It said that since the dawn of time rape has been the inviolable province of the human male.

It said that Myrtle Culpepper was to be applauded in her noble struggle to level this unreasonable barrier.

I gave the coffee back to Betsy.

I said I want to trade this in.

I said on a fifth of Sunnybrook.

I spent the day drinking.

I drank scotch and peppermint schnapps and a fifth of champagne.

I listened to the radio.

Myrtle Culpepper had become a legend in her time.

Myrtle Culpepper fan clubs were springing up like weeds.

The United States Coast Guard band played "The Myrtle Culpepper March."

It sounded a little bit like *Alte Kameraden*.

All except the middle parts.

I watched John Dewberry's five o'clock newscast.

John Dewberry was a darkly handsome man with liberal leanings.

His silver tongue was loose on both ends and hinged in the middle.

John Dewberry stated unequivocally that Myrtle Culpepper was on the right track.

He said that Myrtle Culpepper was a gallant and courageous lady.

He likened her to Carry Nation and Amelia Earhart and Bernadette of Lourdes.

He offered to meet Myrtle Culpepper secretly.

He said he was anxious to get her views on the subject of equal opportunity rape.

He invited her to call him at the television studio immediately.

I spent the evening drinking.

I drank peach brandy and blackberry brandy and apricot brandy and cherry brandy.

I said Betsy do you have any cucumber brandy?

Betsy shook her head.

She said Chance all this drinking can't make things any better.

I said well you may rest assured there is no way it can make them any worse.

Betsy said why don't you put it out of your mind?

She said why don't you just recite "Hats Off the Flag Is Passing By"?

She said or sing "God Bless America."

She said or something.

I didn't answer.

I poured some tequila into a glass of Ovaltine and settled back to watch John Dewberry's ten o'clock newscast.

John Dewberry had nothing to say about the bombing of the Mormon Tabernacle by the Symbionese Liberation Army Air Force.

He avoided mention of the mass suicide of the entire United States Senate.

He ignored the capture of five United States aircraft carriers by a Cambodian rowboat.

John Dewberry got right down to important things.

He announced that he had met secretly with Myrtle Culpepper.

He said that he had learned Myrtle Culpepper's views on the subject of equal opportunity rape.

John Dewberry was missing some hair.

His face was scratched.

His lower lip was swollen.

John Dewberry said that Myrtle Culpepper had been exceedingly difficult to interview.

He declined to discuss certain details of their meeting.

He said that Myrtle Culpepper presented a serious threat to American society.

He added that Myrtle Culpepper would present a serious threat to just about any other society that came readily to mind.

He included those of the African crocodile and the Himalayan abominable snowman.

He said that Myrtle Culpepper was an utterly demented and dangerous female.

He likened her to Lizzie Borden and Lucrezia Borgia and Lady Macbeth.

He apologized to Lucrezia Borgia.

He recommended that the Illinois National Guard be mobilized within the hour.

He further recommended the prompt issue of nuclear weapons.

He apologized to Lady Macbeth.

He broke down and wept.

He said I was given fifteen cents.

He apologized to Lizzie Borden.

He requested his audience to join him in a moment of silent prayer.

He signed off.

I had a double vodka and went to bed.

Betsy had the clock-radio on.

It was playing "The Myrtle Culpepper Tango."

The announcer said that bumper stickers were beginning to appear on cars driven by little old ladies.

He said they read Go Myrtle Go.

I got up and had a glass of gin.

When I came back to bed Betsy said I just heard a news flash.

She said somebody has invented a Myrtle Culpepper doll.

She said you wind it up and it rapes somebody.

> ...oncet I knowed a feller what went
> around impersonating General Custer ...
> got hisself scalped at a Methodist camp
> meeting. ...
>
> MONROE D. UNDERWOOD

❈

By Friday morning my hangover was almost gone.

I drove to the Elmwood Park Post Office and picked up my pay.

From there I went to Wallace's.

Old Dad Underwood was dozing in a booth.

Wallace was studying him with bloodshot eyes.

Wallace glanced at me.

He said do you know that just looking at him gives me a terrible headache?

I said I thought it was the air pollution and them Sox.

Old Dad Underwood stirred.

He yawned and opened one eye.

He gave Wallace a dirty look.

He said you wouldn't know a headache from a ingrown toenail.

Wallace said maybe not but I know a pain in the ass when I see one.

161

Old Dad Underwood said well you got to admit that I am one pain in the ass what ain't never got raped yet.

Wallace gnawed on his raw knuckles.

He said Chance is that goofy old broad still running around loose?

I shrugged.

I said so far as I know.

Wallace shuddered.

Old Dad Underwood climbed out of the booth and sat beside me.

I bought a round.

I said I don't suppose you have ever heard of a Nivlek Ysteb.

Old Dad Underwood said oh sure.

He said you was talking about him just the other day.

He said who is Nivlek Ysteb?

I said Nivlek Ysteb is a big-shot Communist.

Old Dad Underwood shook his head.

He said well you sure ain't going to find no Communists in this neck of the woods.

He said you want to find Communists you got to go down on Armitage Avenue in the thirty-three hunnert block.

He said I ain't never seen so many Communists.

He said why they got more Communists down there than you can shake a stick at.

I said how do you know?

Old Dad Underwood said oh I come by there every so often.

He said there is Communists all over the goddam place.

I said I mean how do you know they are Communists?

Old Dad Underwood shot me a look.

He said they got long hair that's how.

I gave a meaningful whistle.

I said oh my God man you should have told me this earlier.

I said this is valuable information.

Old Dad Underwood put a warning hand on my arm.

He said listen boy you better stay out of there if you don't got long hair.

I said do you have to have long hair to be a Communist?

Old Dad Underwood frowned.

He said well by God that's the funny part.

He said there is short-haired Communists in Russia.

He said even in China.

He said but not on Armitage Avenue.

He said not in the thirty-three hunnert block.

Wallace drifted over with a couple of beers.

He said when I sell this joint I am going to Newfoundland where I will become a fisherman.

He said when you get out on that there ocean you don't get but very little air pollution.

He said and no Sox.

Old Dad Underwood said you going to have to watch out for all them there mermaids.

He said good looking feller like you liable to get hisself raped.

The phone rang.

I knew it was Betsy from the way Wallace blushed.

He handed me the phone.

Betsy said come on home.

She said we are going to have a big fish fry.

I said if you had to have a big fish fry you should have waited.

I said Wallace could have given us one hell of a deal.

I said I'll be there in about forty-five minutes.

I finished my beer.

I drove west to Pulaski Road.

There was a wig shop on the corner.

I bought a long-haired black wig and a drooping black moustache.

I stuffed them into my jacket pocket.

When I got to Betsy's place Mary Bright was walking Bonzo.

Bonzo leered at me.

Mary Bright waved.

I didn't stop.

Bonzo sat down and howled as though his poor heart would break.

On my way up the stairs I put on the wig and moustache.

I knocked on Betsy's door.

When Betsy opened it I hollered down with the imperialistic capitalist whore.

I jumped into the room.

I grabbed Betsy by the throat.

...feeling bad oncet in a while makes feeling good feel even better....

MONROE D. UNDERWOOD

I regained consciousness very slowly.
I was doubled up on the floor.
I was clutching my groin.
I was groaning.
Betsy was holding the ice bag to my head.
I said baby it isn't my head this time.
Betsy said good Lord Chance I didn't know it was you.
I said kung fu you too Betsy.
Betsy said honey I'm sorry.
She said you scared me to death.
She said besides you didn't say call girl.
She said where did you ever get that absolutely ridiculous disguise?
I sat up gingerly.
Betsy said when you feel better I will mix you a nice strong drink.
I said the hell with the nice strong drink.
I said see if you can find a Bible.

. . . any time a feller gets to enjoying store-boughten fish he got to be either crazy or in love. . . .

MONROE D. UNDERWOOD

The fish fry was delicious.
Betsy is the world's greatest cook.
Betsy makes her own tartar sauce.
You got to be awful smart to make your own tartar sauce.

❖

During coffee Betsy started to laugh.

She said you looked like Rasputin with all that crazy hair.

I said I do not know the rock musicians by name.

Betsy said Rasputin is dead.

I said he must have been kicked in the groin.

Betsy said tell me about the wig.

I said well tonight I got to go down to the thirty-three hundred block of Armitage Avenue.

I said there is a whole mess of Communists down there.

I said they all got long hair.

Betsy nodded.

She said of course they do.

She said please excuse me for a moment.

She said I have to make a phone call.

> *...oncet there was a TV station what said
> everything is just dandy ... that night the
> antenna fell down....*
>
> MONROE D. UNDERWOOD

Later on Betsy and I watched a half-hour special on how the mayor was screwing up the city of Chicago.

This was followed by a half-hour special on how the governor was screwing up the state of Illinois.

Then we saw a half-hour special on how the President was screwing up the United States of America.

I got up and slipped into my sports jacket.

I put on my wig and drooping black moustache.

I said I better go.

I said I got a hunch God comes next.

> ... oncet I knowed a feller what swerved
> his car to avoid hitting a polecat ... ran
> over three priests and a rabbi ... just
> missed a couple preachers ... regretted it
> the rest of his life. ...

MONROE D. UNDERWOOD

I spotted the '74 black Mercury when I left the building.

It was parked just north of my car.

There were two guys in it.

Both had beards and moustaches.

They were watching me intently.

I walked to my car.

Nonchalantly.

I got in.

Nonchalantly.

I lit a cigarette.

Nonchalantly.

I started the engine.

I stomped on the accelerator.

Rubber screamed and smoked.

The Olds 98 rocketed away from the curb.

The Mercury got started late but my rear-view mirror showed that it was closing fast.

As I approached Mama Rosa's grocery store I saw Mary Bright's Airedale dash into the street.

I hit the brakes.

The Olds fishtailed.

It went over the curb and onto the sidewalk.

The Mercury sideswiped a tree.

It wiped out a mailbox.

It knocked over a fireplug.

It crashed into Mama Rosa's grocery store.

I heard the sounds of falling glass and a lot of hollering.

Then I heard a lot of hollering and the sounds of falling glass.

I piled out of the Olds.

Water was spurting thirty feet into the air.

Women were screaming.

Babies were crying.

Bonzo was barking.

I headed for Mama Rosa's grocery store.

Mama Rosa was beating the Mercury driver over the head with a pepperoni.

The passenger staggered free of the wreckage.

He jumped through what was left of the plate glass window.

Bonzo was in hot pursuit.

A moment later I heard the passenger yelling *liberare me abietto bestia.*

The driver broke loose from Mama Rosa.

His gray eyes protruded like a grasshopper's.

He demolished a potato chip display.

He went through the door.

He didn't open it.

He lit out for the alley.

I started after him.

I tripped and fell.

I bounced to my feet.

I rounded the corner.

I saw Myrtle Culpepper bring him down with a flying tackle.

I stopped.

Sirens wailed in the distance.

*. . . big difference between getting married
and going to jail is jailhouse coffee ain't
always bad. . . .*

MONROE D. UNDERWOOD

At the Shakespeare police station Kellis J. Ammson was missing some hair.

His face was scratched.

His lower lip was swollen.

He was waving his wig with one hand.

He was waving his phony moustache with the other.

Bits of potato chips rained to the floor.

Kellis J. Ammson mopped his eyes with his wig.

He said officer we were hired to protect this flaming lunatic.

He said oh great flaming God in flaming heaven can you imagine that?

He said like Little Red flaming Hood being hired to protect the flaming wolf.

He said I got raped to boot.

Kellis J. Ammson said she gave me a flaming dime.

Gino Scarletti said I no even getta dime.

The seat of Gino Scarletti's pants was missing.

He was picking glass out of his ears.

He tore off his wig.

He ripped at his walrus moustache.

He shrieked with pain.

He said amma forget thatsa mine.

He said to hell with thissa racket.

He said I know where I getta new job.

He said testa parachutes over shark infesta waters.

He said it ain't good but itsa safer.

I threw my wig and drooping black moustache into a wastebasket.

I shrugged.

I said how could I know it was you guys?

I said you were wearing wigs and moustaches.

I said I thought you were Communists.

I said who hired you?

Kellis J. Ammson said your flaming girl friend the flaming whore.

I grabbed Kellis J. Ammson by the necktie.

I said call girl you ignoramus.

The grizzled old desk sergeant looked up from his crossword puzzle.

He smiled a sad smile.

He said boys it has been just creamy.

He said you have brought sunshine into my drab existence.

He said your antics have warmed my heart.

He said and now you sonsofbitches are going to jail.

He motioned to a couple of cops.

He said throw the happiness boys in the cooler.

He said throw the keys in the lake.

Mama Rosa bailed Gino Scarletti out at eight o'clock.

She took him by the arm.

She said hey kid amma like you fromma start.

Gino Scarletti said somma start.

Mama Rosa said amma gonna give you high-classa
posish.

She said needa man arounda store.

She said odda jobs.

She crushed Gino Scarletti to her enormous bosom.

She said anna things.

Gino Scarletti said anna whatta things?

Mama Rosa said hey kid don't acta dumb.

174

She led him away.

He went docilely.

Betsy bailed me out at ten o'clock.

That left Kellis J. Ammson.

Kellis J. Ammson rattled his cell door in the manner of a circus gorilla.

He said &@#$%¢*!

The grizzled old desk sergeant said don't rattle that door and stop saying &@#$%¢*!

He said profanity is the clamoring of the limited intellect.

Kellis J. Ammson said I wish to announce that I am not favorably impressed with the recent flaming course of flaming events.

He said I predict sweeping flaming changes in the immediate flaming future.

I waved to Ammson.

I said I'll send the flaming Salvation Army band.

I said I'll have it play "The Myrtle Culpepper Lullaby."

Kellis J. Ammson said go jump in bed with your flaming whore.

The grizzled old desk sergeant said call girl you flaming barbarian.

Betsy's car was parked around the corner.

I said what took you so long?

Betsy said I had a call.

I said I didn't know you serviced the Schenectady area.

Betsy said Chance why don't you drop this crazy case?

I said how can I drop it?

I said I'm working for the government.

I said I got to find that goddam Nivlek Ysteb.

Betsy sighed.

She said but you aren't finding Nivlek Ysteb.

She said all you are doing is pounding lumps on Ammson and Scarletti.

I said that don't make me a bad guy.

I said how come you hired those clowns?

Betsy said I was trying to keep you from getting hurt.

As we drove away Betsy said what are you staring at?

I said I thought I saw Myrtle Culpepper in that doorway across the street.

When we got home the phone was ringing.
Betsy answered it.
She said oh yes just a moment please.
She glanced anxiously in my direction.
She said Chance I'm simply parched.
She said would you get me a bottle of orange soda
from the refrigerator?
When I came back Betsy had hung up.
She said sweetie I have a hurry-up appointment.
I shrugged.
I said okay.
I said what the hell.
I said don't worry about me kiddo.
I said I got to finish a story in *Eagles* magazine.
I said besides I'm pretty tired.
Betsy said don't be mad.
I said who's mad?
I said everything is peaches.

I said life is just a great big bowl of raspberries.
Betsy left without touching her orange soda.
I sat on the couch and smoked a few cigarettes.
I turned the radio on.
I heard "The Myrtle Culpepper Boogie."
I turned the radio off.
I turned the record player on.
Alte Kameraden didn't help.
I went to bed.
It was a rotten world.

*. . . sex is something you can't put back
where you got it. . . .*

MONROE D. UNDERWOOD

❈

Betsy came in shortly after four.
I felt her get into bed.
We didn't touch each other.
After daylight I heard the phone ring a couple of times.
At ten o'clock Betsy shook me awake.
Very gently.
I said what's up?
Betsy said Old Dad Underwood was tending bar at
Wallace's last night.
I said Betsy did you wake me up to tell me that?
Betsy said he was raped by Myrtle Culpepper.
She said Myrtle Culpepper left him five hundred dol-
lars.
I said well what's he bitching about?
I said he had a lot better night than I did.
I said is he all right?
Betsy said oh sure.

She said he has fallen head-over-heels in love with Myrtle Culpepper.

She said he is writing a song about her.

She said he says it will be better than "When the Golden Beer is Foaming in Wyoming."

I said that's great.

I said they were made for each other.

I went back to sleep.

> *... oncet I knowed a good whore what*
> *went straight ... three hunnert fellers had*
> *to start sleeping with their wives ... it was*
> *a most tragic period. ...*

MONROE D. UNDERWOOD

I got up at noon.

Betsy said don't you want something besides a cup of black coffee?

I said in a few minutes.

Betsy said then what?

I said another cup of black coffee.

I was looking at the morning Chicago *Sun-Times*.

It said that Myrtle Culpepper had raped a veteran desk sergeant at the Shakespeare police station late last night.

It said she had left him a crossword-puzzle book.

It said that the veteran desk sergeant had announced his retirement from the police force effective immediately.

It quoted him as saying &@ #$%¢*!

It mentioned that he had been through a lot recently.

It said that he planned to spend his retirement years somewhere south of the South Pole.

I dug a pack of Camels out of my bathrobe pocket.

I gave one to Betsy.

We lit up.

Betsy didn't blow any smoke rings.

I said you were acting mighty strange last night.

I said do you want to tell me about it?

Betsy nodded in slow motion.

She stared into her coffee cup.

Without looking up she said Chance do you remember what you told me the other evening?

I shrugged.

I said what other evening?

Betsy said the evening of the storm.

I said we were talking about *Eagles* magazine.

Betsy said now Chance Purdue you just cut that out.

She said you told me you would marry me as soon as you caught up with Nivlek Ysteb.

I said oh that.

Betsy looked up.

She said did you mean it?

I shrugged.

I said I guess.

Betsy said wait a minute.

She said you guess?

I said okay I meant it.

I said of course there is still that minor matter of locating good old Nivlek.

I smiled like a leopard in a canary hatchery.

Betsy winked at me.

She mimicked my smile.

She leaned forward.

She dangled her left hand under my nose.

She said big boy you better know where you can buy a wedding ring in one hell of a hurry.

She winked at me.

She said Chance I can give you Nivlek Ysteb in five minutes.

She winked at me again.

I said I didn't think you drank this early in the day.

182

I said that's probably what is wrong with your eye.

Betsy said so now we will be married at last.

She said it's about time goddammit.

She clasped her hands and squeezed until her knuckles turned white.

She said oh Chance it will be wonderful.

She said we will enter different professions.

She said we will grow old together you and I.

I said if we enter different professions we will not get a chance to grow old together you and I.

I said this is because we will starve to death together you and I.

Betsy said the hell we will.

I said you seem pretty certain of yourself.

Betsy said you won't chicken out?

I said I never chicken out.

Betsy gave me a long unblinking look.

She said so be it then.

She got up and marched purposefully out of the kitchen.

When she returned she handed me a sheet of stationery and a ball-point pen.

The pen advertised the Kellis J. Ammson Private Detective Agency.

Betsy's hands were trembling.

She said well sweetheart here goes the old ball game.

She said what's my name?

I said I just chickened out.

I said I'm not marrying no broad who got amnesia.

Betsy said print my name on that sheet of paper.

Now print the name of my street.

She said now turn the paper over and hold it to the light.

She said what do you see?

I said I see a whole bunch of upside-down letters.

Betsy said no no no.

She said turn the paper the other way.

She said now what do you see?

I said I see a whole bunch of backwards letters.

Betsy said read as though the letters aren't backwards.

I did.

I could feel the blood drain from my face.

I dropped the sheet of paper.

It floated to the floor.

I got up and took a can of beer from the refrigerator.

I went into the living room.

The radio was playing "The Myrtle Culpepper Rhapsody."

I sat on the couch.

There was deathly quiet in the kitchen.

In a few minutes Betsy came in.

She sat beside me.

Her eyes were red.

She said Chance believe me this isn't as bad as it looks.

She said I wasn't trying to make a fool of you.

I laughed wildly.

Betsy said I was afraid I was losing you to Candi Yakozi.

She said I had to do something.

I said that's what the man said after he threw gasoline on the fire.

Betsy said I just wanted you to live with me.

She said I thought I could make you happy.

She said I hoped you might come to like it.

She buried her face in her hands.

She sobbed like a baby.

She said I've blown it.

She said &@#$%¢*!

I said stop crying and don't say &@#$%¢*!

I said I'm not marrying no broad who is always crying and saying &@#$%¢*!

Betsy peeped at me from between her fingers.

She said you'll still marry me?

I said I guess I better.

I said I got to get you off the market.

I said you pull one like this on some other guy and he will kill you in cold blood.

Betsy said I don't want some other guy.

She said you're the only guy I ever wanted.

I said who was that fake government sonofabitch?

Betsy frowned.

She said oh yes.

She said I forget his name now that you bring him to mind.

She said he was sort of expensive as I recall.

She said he was an unemployed TV actor or something.

She said I think he was a doctor in "Heartbreak Hospital" for a short time.

I said if I ever see him again he will be a patient in the Mayo Clinic for a long time.

I said I wonder which half I should send to Mayo.

I said all right let's get at it.

I said when do you want to get married?

Betsy said right after we buy Wallace's tavern.

I said I just chickened out again.

I said I'm not marrying no broad who gets hallucinations.

I said Wallace will never sell.

Betsy said honey I met with Wallace last night.

She said do you want to see an option to buy?

I shrugged.

I said what do we use for money?

Betsy said a wedding gift from Kellis J. Ammson.

I said Ammson wouldn't come up with a wedding gift for the bride of Frankenstein.

I said even if he was Frankenstein.

I said which is a distinct possibility.

Betsy said I met with Ammson last night too.

She said right after he got out of jail.

She said do you want to see a check?

I shrugged.

Betsy said he even let me keep the ball-point pen.

I said what does Ammson get out of this?

Betsy said absolutely nothing but your sworn statement that you will never practice as a private investigator within thirteen thousand miles of Chicago.

She said it must be written in blood of course.

I said oh certainly.

I said how else?

I said &@#$%¢*!

Betsy said stop saying &@#$%¢*!

She said it isn't polite.

I said I am going to write a book about this.

I said it will be a mystery.

I said I will call it *Nivlek Ysteb Who the Hell are You?*

I said or maybe *The DADA Caper*.

Betsy giggled and dried her eyes.

She said will you employ a *nom de plume?*

I said no I intend to keep it as clean as possible.

I said but I will use somebody else's name.

I said maybe I will call myself Ross H. Spencer.

I said he can't write either.

Betsy shook her head.

She said it won't work.

She said the average reader will solve it by page 80.

I said oh I don't know about that.

I said it took me clear to page 184.

I said and I'm a detective.

Betsy said not any longer.

She said you are about to become a tavern proprietor.

Betsy was staring at me with those big pale blue eyes.

Like a kid stares at a new bicycle.

She looked small and helpless and beautiful.

I took her in my arms.

I kissed her.

From the bottom of my heart.

The phone rang.

Betsy said let it ring.

I said not on your life.

I said this is the end of the call girl trail.

Betsy said oh my God for once you didn't say whore.

I grabbed the phone.

Candi Yakozi said is Betsy there?

I said no.

Candi Yakozi said oh goody goody.

I said I am here with Nivlek Ysteb.

I said I thought I was stalking Nivlek Ysteb.

I said all the time Nivlek Ysteb was stalking me.

Candi Yakozi said oh Jesus shall I call the cops?

I said no it's much too late for that.

Candi Yakozi said well come around any old time.

I hung up.

Betsy said who was that?

I said that was Idnac Izokay.

Betsy said Idnac Izowho?

I said never mind.

I said I probably mispronounced it anyway.

I said I never was good at names.

The radio was playing "The Myrtle Culpepper Serenade."

Winston was looking through the window at me.

His head was cocked quizzically.

A tiny teardrop rolled down his cheek.

I said Betsy Winston is crying.

Betsy said birds don't cry.

Winston turned his back to me.

He flew away.

I watched him until he was a tiny dot in the cloudless blue sky.

I wiped my eyes with the back of my hand.

I think he was disappointed in me.

CHICAGO, Oct. 9 — A terrified man stumbled into Chicago FBI headquarters late yesterday afternoon and offered valuable information in return for what he called "sexual asylum." He represented himself as being the leader of a vast subversive network dedicated to the destruction of the United States. He claimed to be a native of Brussels. He is undergoing psychiatric tests here prior to being flown to Washington for interrogation by intelligence experts.

Government spokesmen withheld the identity of the man but confirmed the existence of an organization similar to that described by him. Some bystanders said that the man was missing some hair and others noted that he had a scratched face and a swollen lower lip. He was nearly penniless except for a crumpled ten-dollar bill on which the picture of Alexander Hamilton bore a bright red moustache.

It is theorized that the man was once employed by a New York municipal service because the pocket of his shirt carried a monogram consisting of the letters NY.

As he was led to a security area the unidentified man waved a tiny American flag and sang "God Bless America."

DADA

(DESTROY AMERICA DESTROY AMERICA)

"They must be serious,
they said it twice."

Narration . . . . .Chance Purdue
Sagacious comments . . Old Dad Underwood
Typing . . . . .Betsy Purdue

AVON ⬡ THE BEST IN
BESTSELLING ENTERTAINMENT!

- [ ] **Your Erroneous Zones**
  Dr. Wayne W. Dyer — 33373 — $2.25
- [ ] **Ghost Fox**   James Houston — 35733 — $1.95
- [ ] **Ambassador**   Stephen Longstreet — 31997 — $1.95
- [ ] **The Boomerang Conspiracy**
  Michael Stanley — 35535 — $1.95
- [ ] **Gypsy Lady**   Shirlee Busbee — 36145 — $1.95
- [ ] **Good Evening Everybody**
  Lowell Thomas — 35105 — $2.25
- [ ] **Jay J. Armes, Investigator**
  Jay J. Armes and Frederick Nolan — 36494 — $1.95
- [ ] **The Mists of Manitoo**
  Lois Swann — 33613 — $1.95
- [ ] **Flynn**   Gregory Mcdonald — 34975 — $1.95
- [ ] **Lovefire**   Julia Grice — 34538 — $1.95
- [ ] **Hollywood Is a Four Letter Town**
  James Bacon — 33399 — $1.95
- [ ] **Mystic Rose**   Patricia Gallagher — 33381 — $1.95
- [ ] **The Search for Joseph Tully**
  William H. Hallahan — 33712 — $1.95
- [ ] **Starring**   James Fritzhand — 33118 — $1.95
- [ ] **Legacy**   Florence Hurd — 33480 — $1.95
- [ ] **Delta Blood**   Barbara Ferry Johnson — 32664 — $1.95
- [ ] **Wicked Loving Lies**   Rosemary Rogers — 30221 — $1.95
- [ ] **Moonstruck Madness**   Laurie McBain — 31385 — $1.95
- [ ] **ALIVE: The Story of the Andes Survivors**
  Piers Paul Read — 21535 — $1.95
- [ ] **Sweet Savage Love**   Rosemary Rogers — 28027 — $1.95
- [ ] **The Flame and the Flower**
  Kathleen E. Woodiwiss — 35485 — $2.25
- [ ] **I'm OK—You're OK**
  Thomas A. Harris, M.D. — 28282 — $2.25

Available at better bookstores everywhere, or order direct from the publisher.

AVON BOOKS, Mail Order Dept., 250 West 55th St., New York, N.Y. 10019

Please send me the books checked above. I enclose $_____(please include 25¢ per copy for postage and handling). Please use check or money order—sorry, no cash or COD's. Allow 4-6 weeks for delivery.

Mr/Mrs/Miss_____

Address_____

City_____State/Zip_____

BBBB 2-78

THE EXPLOSIVE N...
THE AUTHOR...
CONFES...

FLYNN

He's a tough-talking Boston cop, a family man whose daughter just got a ruby pin from a guy named Fletch, and whose son was just fleeced of a violin.

FLYNN

And there they are, talking about rubies and violins when a plane explodes overhead. Burning bodies fall out of the sky— 118 of them!

FLYNN

Aboard the plane were a Federal judge, a British actor, a middleweight champ, an Arab potentate—and, wouldn't you know it, a case for the formidable Flynn.

FLYNN

"Flynn is one of the smartest, gentlest, most sarcastic cops you'll ever meet."

The New York Times

FLYNN

BY GREGORY MCDONALD
TWICE WINNER OF THE
EDGAR AWARD FOR MYSTERY

 Avon 34975 $1.95

FLYNN 10-77